"Look at me," she ordered. "You know me, Luc."

Blowing out a breath, Luc hung his head. "I... It's on the tip of my tongue. Damn, why can't I remember?" Worry filled his dark eyes.

This was not good, not good at all. She was going to have to get her boss back to the house and call the palace doctor. Obviously Luc's memory wasn't cooperating if he couldn't remember that they worked together. But she didn't want him panicking; she could do that enough for both of them.

"My name is Kate." She watched his eyes, hoping to see some recognition, but there was nothing. "I'm your—"

"Fiancée." A wide smile spread across his face. "Now I remember."

Before she could correct him, Luc leaned in to capture her lips with a passion she'd never known before.

A ROYAL
AMNESIA SCANDAL

BY
JULES BENNETT

Published in Great Britain 2015
by Mills & Boon, an imprint of Harlequin (UK) Limited,
Eton House, 18-24 Paradise Road, Richmond, Surrey, TW9 1SR

© 2015 Jules Bennett

ISBN: 978-0-263-25847-9

Harlequin (UK) Limited's policy is to use papers that are natural, renewable and recyclable products and made from wood grown in sustainable forests. The lo_____ nmental regula____

Printe___
by CP___

Award-winning author **Jules Bennett** is no stranger to romance—she met her husband when she was only fourteen. After dating through high school, the two married. He encouraged her to chase her dream of becoming an author. Jules has now published nearly thirty novels. She and her husband are living their own happily-ever-after while raising two girls. Jules loves to hear from readers through her website, www.julesbennett.com, her Facebook fan page or on Twitter.

I have to dedicate this book to the fabulous
Andrea Laurence and Sarah M. Anderson
who always come through for me when I need a plot
fixed five minutes ago. Wouldn't go through
this crazy journey without you guys!

One

Escaping to the mountains would have been much better for his sanity than coming to his newly purchased private seaside villa off the coast of Portugal.

Kate Barton fully clothed was enough to have any man panting, but Kate running around in a bikini with some flimsy, strapless wrap that knotted right at her cleavage was damn near crippling. The woman had curves, she wasn't stick-thin like a model and damn if she didn't know how to work those dips and valleys on that killer body. Not that she ever purposely showcased herself, at least not in the professional setting, but she couldn't hide what she'd been blessed with, either. Even in a business suit, she rocked any designer's label.

Luc Silva cursed beneath his breath as he pulled his Jet Ski back to the dock and secured it. His intent in coming here was to escape from the media, escape from the woman who'd betrayed him. So why was he paying a penance with yet another woman?

To ensure privacy for both of them, he'd given Kate the guesthouse. Unfortunately, it and the main house shared the same private beach, damn it. He'd thought purchasing this fixer-upper on a private island, barely up to civilization's standards, was a brilliant idea at the time. With no internet access and little cell service, it was a perfect hideaway for a member of Ilha Beleza's royal family. He didn't want to be near people who knew of or cared about his status. Luc had only one requirement when searching for a hideout: a place to escape. Yet here he was with his sexy, mouthy, curvy assistant.

Not only that, the renovations to the property were only half-done, because he'd needed to get away from reality much sooner than he'd thought he would.

A lying fiancée would do that to a man.

"Your face is burning."

Luc fisted his hands at his sides as he approached Kate. Was she draped all over that lounge chair on purpose or did she just naturally excel at tormenting men? She'd untied that wrap and now it lay open, as if framing her luscious body covered only by triangles of bright red material and strings.

"I'm not burned," he retorted, not slowing down as he marched up the white sand.

"Did you apply sunscreen?" she asked, holding an arm over her forehead to shield her eyes from the sun.

The movement shifted her breasts, and the last thing he needed was to be staring at his assistant's chest, no matter how impressive it was. When she'd started working for him about a year ago, he'd wanted her… He still wanted her, if he was being honest with himself.

She was the absolute best assistant he'd ever had. Her parents still worked for his parents, so hiring Kate had been an easy decision.

A decision he questioned every single time his hormones shot into overdrive when she neared.

He never mingled with staff. He and his parents always kept their personal and professional relationships separate, so as not to create bad press or scandal. It was a rule they felt very strongly about after a scandal generations ago. Rumor had it the family was quite the center of gossip for a while after an assistant let out family secrets best left behind closed doors.

So once Luc had become engaged to Alana, he'd put his attraction to Kate out of his mind.

For the past three months, he'd been ready to say "I do" for two very valid reasons: his ex had claimed to be expecting his child, and he needed to marry to secure his crown to reign over Ilha Beleza.

Now Alana was gone and he was trying like hell to hang on to the title, even though he had just a few months to find a wife. And the second he was in charge, he'd be changing that archaic law. Just because a man was nearing thirty-five didn't mean he had to be tied down, and Luc wanted nothing to do with holy matrimony… especially now that he'd been played.

"You're frowning," Kate called as he passed right by her. "Being angry isn't helping your red face."

There were times he admired the fact she didn't treat him as if he was royalty, but just a regular man. This wasn't one of those times.

Before climbing the steps to the outdoor living area, Luc turned. "Did you cancel the interview with that journalist from the States?"

Kate settled back into her relaxed position, dropping her arm to her side and closing her eyes as the sun continued to kiss all that exposed skin.

"I took care of canceling all media interviews you

had scheduled regarding the upcoming wedding, or anything to do with Alana," she told him. "I rescheduled your one-on-one interviews for later in the year, after you gain the title. By then I'm positive you'll have everything sorted out and will be at the top of your game."

Luc swallowed. Not only was Kate his right-hand woman, she was his biggest supporter and advocate. She made him look good to the media, occasionally embellishing the truth to further boost his family's name.

"I simply told each of the media outlets that this was a difficult time for you, playing up the faux miscarriage, and your family's request for privacy."

Kate lifted a knee, causing a little roll of skin to ease over her bikini bottoms. Luc's eyes instantly went to that region of her body and he found himself wanting to drop to his knees and explore her with more than his eyes.

"If you're done staring at me, you need to either go inside or put on sunscreen," she added, without opening her eyes.

"If you'd cover up, I wouldn't stare."

Her soft laugh, drifting on an ocean breeze, hit him square in the gut. "If I covered up, I wouldn't get a tan. Be glad I'm at least wearing this. I do hate those tan lines."

Gritting his teeth, Luc tried but failed at keeping that mental image from his mind. Kate sunbathing in the nude would surely have any man down on his knees begging. Forcing back a groan, Luc headed up the steps and into the main house. She was purposely baiting him, and he was letting her, because he was at a weak spot in his life right now. He also couldn't hide the fact that his assistant turned him inside out in ways she shouldn't.

He'd been engaged, for pity's sake, yet before and after the engagement, he'd wanted to bed Kate.

Sleeping with an employee was beyond tacky, and he wasn't going to be so predictable as to fall into that cliché. Besides, the house rule of no fraternizing with employees was something he stood behind wholeheartedly.

He and Kate were of like minds, and they needed to remain in a professional relationship. Period. Kate stood up for him, stood by him, no matter what, and he refused to risk that by jumping into bed with her.

She had been just as shocked as he was when Alana's deception had been revealed. For once, Kate hadn't made a snarky comment, hadn't tried to be cute or funny. She'd instantly intervened, taking all calls, offering up reasons why the engagement had been called off.

In fact, it was Kate's brilliant plan that had saved his pride. She'd informed the media that Alana had miscarried, and the couple had opted to part ways as friends. At first he'd wanted to just come out with the truth, but he'd been so hurt by the personal nature of the lie, he'd gone along with the farce to save face.

So, for all the times Kate got under his skin with their verbal sparring and her torturous body, he couldn't manage this situation without her.

There were times, even before the fiancée debacle, that he'd just wished he had a place to run to and escape all the chaos of being royalty. Purchasing this home— even though it needed some updating—was like a gift to himself. The view had sold him immediately. With the infinity pool overlooking the Mediterranean Sea and the lush gardens, the previous owners obviously had to have been outdoor enthusiasts. At least Luc had a dock for his Jet Ski and his boat.

Too bad he'd had to come here before all the remodeling was complete. Kate had informed the workers they would have the next two weeks off because the house would be in use. The contractors had managed to get a few of the rooms fully renovated, and thankfully, Luc's master suite was one of them.

He stripped off his wet trunks and stepped into his glass-enclosed shower, which gave the illusion of being outside, but in fact was surrounded by lush tropical plants. The shower was an addition to the master suite and one of his favorite features in the house. He loved having the feeling of being outdoors while being ensured of the privacy he craved. That had been his top priority when he'd bought the house.

An image of sharing this spacious shower with Kate slammed into his mind, and Luc had to focus on something else. Such as the fact she was ten years younger than him, and when he'd been learning to drive, she'd been going to kindergarten and losing her first tooth. There. That should make him feel ridiculous about having such carnal thoughts toward his assistant…shouldn't it?

Water sluiced over his body as he braced his hands against the glass wall and leaned forward. Dropping his head, he contemplated all the reasons why bedding his assistant was wrong. Not only would things be awkward between them, but any bad press could threaten his ascension to the throne. Not to mention the no-fraternization rule, which had been implemented for a reason. He didn't want to be the cause for a black mark on his family's name. One major issue was all he could handle right now. Unfortunately, the one and only reason for wanting to claim her kept trumping all the mounting negatives. He had to find a way to keep her at arm's length, because if he kept seeing her parading around in that skimpy gear, he'd never make it through these next two weeks alone with her.

Scrolling through the upcoming schedule, Kate jotted down the important things she needed to follow up on once she was back at the Land of the Internet, aka the palace. Even though Luc was taking a break from life, she had no such luxury, with or without cyberspace. He might be reeling from the embarrassment of the breakup, and dodging the media's speculations, but she still had to stay one step ahead of the game in order to keep him pristine in the eyes of the people once the dust cloud of humiliation settled. Damage control had moved to the top of her priorities in her role as assistant.

Being the assistant to a member of the royal family hadn't been her childhood aspiration. Granted, he wasn't just any member of the royal family, but the next king of Ilha Beleza, but still.

At one time Kate had had notions of being a dress designer. She'd watched her mother, the royal seamstress, often enough, and admired how she could be so creative and still enjoy her work. But Kate's aspirations hit the wall of reality when she'd discovered she excelled at organizing, being in the thick of business and playing the peacemaker. The job appealed to the do-gooder in her, too, as she felt she could make a real difference in the lives of others.

Once she'd received her degree, Kate knew she wanted to work with the royal family she'd known her entire life. She loved them, loved what they stood for, and she wanted to continue to be in that inner circle.

Kate had first met Luc when she was six and he was sixteen. After that, she'd seen him at random times when she'd go to work with her parents. As Kate grew older and well into her teens, Luc had become more and more appealing to her on every level a woman starts to recognize. Of course, with the age gap, he'd paid her no mind, and she would watch as he'd parade women in and out of the palace.

She'd never thought he would settle down, but as his coronation fast approached, with his thirty-fifth birthday closing in, the timing of Alana's "pregnancy" couldn't have been better.

Too bad the spoiled debutante had had her hopes of being a queen shattered, tarnishing the tiara she would never wear. Alana had tricked Luc into believing she was expecting their child, which was absurd, because there's only so long that lie could go on. Alana hadn't planned on Luc being a hands-on type of father, so when he'd accompanied her to a doctor's appointment, he'd been stunned to realize there was no baby.

At least now Kate wouldn't have to field calls for "Lukey" when he was in meetings and unable to talk. Kate was glad Miss D Cup was out of the picture...not that there was room in the picture for Kate herself, but having that woman around had seriously kept her in a bad mood for the past several months.

As she glanced over Luc's schedule after this two-week hiatus, all she saw was meetings with dignitaries, meetings with his staff, the wedding ceremony and the ball to celebrate the nuptials of his best friend, Mikos Alexander, and a few outings that were just "spontane-ous" enough for the media to snap pictures but not get close enough to question Luc. A quick wave as he en-tered a building, a flash of that dimpled grin to the cam-era, and the paparazzi would be foaming at the mouth to post the shots with whatever captions they chose.

For the past year Kate had tried to get him to take

on charity projects, not for the media hype, but because he had the power to make things happen. Good things, things that would make a difference in people's lives. What good was power and money if they weren't used to help those less fortunate?

But Luc's focus had always been on the crown, on the bigger prize, on his country and what it would take to rule. He wasn't a jerk, but his focus was not on the little guys, which occasionally made Kate's job of making him look like a knight in shining armor a little harder.

Still, working for a royal family had its perks, and she would have to be dead to ignore how sexy her boss was. Luc would make any woman smile with a fantasy-style sigh. But no matter how attractive the man was, Kate prided herself on remaining professional.

She may have daydreamed about kissing him once. Okay, fine. Once a day, but still. Acting on her attraction would be a colossal mistake. Everyone knew the royal family's rules about not fraternizing with staff. The consequences could mean not only her job, but also her parents'. A risk Kate couldn't take, no matter what she ached for.

With a sigh, Kate rose to her feet and set her day planner aside. Luc had warned her that she'd be "roughing it" at this guesthouse, but she sort of liked the basic charm of the place. The rooms were pretty much bare, the scarred hardwood floors desperately in need of refinishing and the kitchen was at least thirty years out of date, if not more. But she was in her own space and had water, electric power and a beach. She wasn't working nearly as much as she had been at the palace in the midst of wedding-planning chaos. All of those media interviews had been canceled or rescheduled, and she was on a secluded island with her hunky boss. So roughing it wasn't so "rough" in her opinion.

Kate headed out her back door, breathing in the fresh scent of the salty ocean breeze. Following the stone path lined with overgrown bushes and lush plants, which led to the main house, she was glad she'd come along even if the circumstances made Luc only edgier, grouchier and, well, difficult. He had every right to be furious and hurt, though he'd never admit to the pain. Luc always put up a strong front, hiding behind that tough-guy persona.

Kate knew better, but she still chose to refrain from discussing the incident too much. Keeping things more professional than personal was the only way she could continue to work for him and not get swept away by lustful feelings.

When Kate had first started working for Luc, they'd had a heated discussion that led to a near kiss before he'd pulled back. He'd informed her right then that under no circumstances did he bed, date or get involved with employees.

Still, long nights spent working together, trips abroad and even the close quarters of his office had led to heated glances and accidental brushes against each other. The attraction most definitely wasn't one-sided.

Then he'd started dating Miss D Cup, and the obvious physical attraction between boss and employee had faded…at least on Luc's side. Typical playboy behavior. Kate had chided herself for even thinking they would eventually give in to that underlying passion.

Yet here they were again, both single and utterly alone. So now more than ever she needed to exercise this ability to remain professional. In reality, she'd love nothing more than to rip those designer clothes off him and see if he had any hidden tan lines or tattoos, because that one on his back that scrolled across his taut muscles and up onto his left shoulder was enough to have her lady parts standing at attention each time he took his shirt off.

As tempted as she was to give in to her desires, too much was at stake: her job, her parents' jobs, the reputation she'd carry of seducing her boss. That wouldn't look good on a résumé.

Kate had left her phone behind and contemplated changing. But since she was comfortable and would be only a minute with Luc—five at the most—she wanted to see if he'd take her up on this venture she'd been requesting his help with for the past year. Now that his life was turned inside out, perhaps he'd be a little more giving of his time.

With her sandals slapping against the stone pathway, Kate rehearsed in her head everything she wanted to say as she made her way to the house, passing by the picturesque infinity pool.

The rear entrance faced the Mediterranean. Of course, there wasn't a bad view from any window or balcony that she'd seen, and her guest cottage was definitely on her list of places she never wanted to leave. Regardless of the updates that needed to be done, this house was gorgeous and would be even more so once Luc's plans were fully executed.

When she reached the glass double doors, she tapped her knuckles against the frame. The ocean breeze lifted her hair, sending it dancing around her shoulders, tickling her skin. The wind had kicked up in the past several minutes and dark clouds were rolling in.

Storms…she loved them. Kate smiled up at the ominous sky and welcomed the change. There was something so sexy and powerful about the recklessness of a thunderstorm.

When she knocked again and Luc still didn't answer, she held her hand to the glass and peered inside. No Luc in sight. The knob turned easily and she stepped inside the spacious living area. It led straight into the kitchen, which was only slightly more modern than hers. Basically, the main house looked the same as the cottage, only supersized, with the entire back wall made up of windows and French doors.

"Luc?" she called, hoping he'd hear her and she wouldn't startle him.

What if he'd decided to rest? Or what if he was in the shower?

A smile spread across her face. Oh, yeah. What if he *was* in the shower? Water sliding over all those glorious tanned muscles…

Down, girl.

She wasn't here to seduce her boss. She was here to plant a seed about a charity project close to her heart. If Luc thought he'd formulated the plan, then he'd be all for it, and she desperately wanted him to donate his time and efforts to an orphanage in the United States she'd been corresponding with on his behalf. For reasons he didn't need to know about, the place held a special spot in her heart. She didn't want him to go there out of pity. She wanted him to do so on his own, because he felt it was the right thing to do.

But Kate couldn't get the twins who lived there, Carly and Thomas, out of her mind, and she was driving herself crazy with worry. For now, though, things were out of her control, so she had to focus on getting Luc on board with funding and volunteering. What would that little bit hurt him, anyway? In all reality, the visit and the monetary gift wouldn't leave a dent in his time or finances, but both would mean the world to those children.

"Luc?" She headed toward the wide, curved staircase with its scrolled, wrought-iron railing. She rested her hand on the banister, only to have it wobble beneath her palm. Definitely another item for the list of renovations.

She didn't even know what room he'd opted to use as the master suite, as there was one downstairs and one upstairs. "Are you up there?" she called, more loudly this time.

Within seconds, Luc stood at the top of the stairs, wearing only a tan and a towel. Kate had seen him in swimming trunks, knew full well just how impressive his body was. Yet standing here looking up at him, knowing there was only a piece of terry cloth and a few stairs between them, sent her hormones into overdrive. And she had to keep reminding herself she was only his assistant.

Still, that wouldn't stop her from appreciating the fact her boss was one fine man. Her "office view" was hands down the best she could ever ask for.

"I'm sorry," she said, forcing her gaze to stay on his face. If she looked away she'd appear weak, as if she couldn't handle seeing a half-naked man. If her eyes lowered to the flawless chest on display, he'd know all her fantasies for sure. "I'll just wait until you're dressed."

Before she made a fool of herself by staring, babbling or drooling, Kate turned and scurried back to the living area, where she sank onto the old sofa that had been draped with a pale yellow cover until the renovations were completed and new furniture arrived. Dropping her head against the saggy cushion, she let out a groan.

Lucas Silva was one *atraente* prince. Sexy prince. After living in Ilha Beleza for a full year now, she was growing more accustomed to thinking in Portuguese as opposed to English. Even thinking of Luc in another language only proved how pathetic she was.

Get a grip.

She should've waited in the living room, or just come back later after her walk. Then she wouldn't have been tortured by seeing him wearing nothing but that towel and the water droplets that clung to those taut muscles. Had he been standing closer, the temptation to lick away all the moisture from his recent shower might have been too much to handle.

She'd held on to her self-control for a year and didn't intend to let it snap now. A man like Luc would enjoy that too much, and Kate refused to be like all the other women who fawned over the playboy prince.

Smoothing her floral, halter-style sundress, she crossed her legs, hoping for a casual look instead of the assistant-hot-for-her-boss one. The second she heard his feet crossing the floor, she sat up straighter and silently scolded herself for allowing her thoughts and hormones to control her.

"Sorry I interrupted your shower," she told him the second he stepped down into the sunken living area. "I was heading out for a walk, but I wanted to run something by you first."

He'd thrown on black board shorts and a red T-shirt. Still, the image of him wearing next to nothing was burned into her mind, and that's all she could focus on. Luc fully or even partially clothed was sexy, but Luc practically in his birthday suit was a much more dangerous thought.

"I'm not working, if that's what you want to discuss." He strode across the room and opened the patio doors, pushing them wide to allow the ocean breeze to stream in. Kate came to her feet, ready to be firm, but careful not to anger him, because this project was too important to her.

"It's just something you need to think about," she retorted as she went to stand near the open doors. "I know we've discussed charity work in the past—"

He turned, held up a hand to cut her off. "I'm not scheduling anything like that until I have the crown. I don't want to even think beyond right now. I've got a big enough mess on my hands."

Crossing her arms, Kate met his gaze...until that gaze dropped to her chest. Well, well, well. Looked as if maybe he wasn't immune to the physical attraction between them, after all.

"I was working on your schedule for the next several months and you have a gap that I could squeeze something into, but you have to be in agreement."

The muscles in his jaw clenched as Kate waited for a response. Whenever he stared at her with such intensity, she never knew what was going through his mind. If his thoughts had anything to do with the way he'd been staring at her moments ago, she was totally on board. Sign her up.

Before she realized what he was doing, Luc reached out and slid a fingertip across her bare shoulder. It took every bit of her willpower not to shiver beneath such a simple, yet intimate touch.

"Wh-what are you doing?" she asked, cursing the stammer.

When his finger trailed across her collarbone, then back to her shoulder, Kate continued to stare, unsure what he was doing. If he was trying to seduce her, he needn't try any harder. With the way he kept looking at her, she was about to throw out the window all the reasons they shouldn't be together. One jerk of the knot of fabric at her neck and that halter dress would slide to the floor.

She waited, more than ready for Luc to make her fantasy come true.

Two

Luc fisted his hands at his sides. What the hell had he been thinking, reaching out and touching Kate like that? He was nothing but a *tolo*, a fool, even to allow himself the brief pleasure.

With all Kate's creamy skin exposed, silently inviting his touch, his last thread of willpower had snapped. And as much as he hated to admit it, even to himself, he was too emotionally drained to think straight. Part of him just wanted someone as a sexual outlet, an escape, but he wouldn't use his assistant...no matter how tempted he was.

Luc hadn't tried hard enough to keep himself in check, which was the main problem. He was still reeling from the fact that Kate had stood at the base of the steps looking as if she might leap to the second floor and devour him if he even hinted he was ready. And *misericórdia*, mercy, he was ready for some no-strings affection. Still, not with his employee. How did this number-one rule keep slipping from his mind?

"You're burned," he replied, surprised when his tone came out stronger than he'd intended. "Looks like you should've taken your own advice about that sunscreen."

With a defiant tilt of her chin, a familiar gesture he'd come to find amusing, she propped her hands on her hips, which did amazing things to the pull of the fabric across her chest. The woman was slowly killing him.

The no-dating-staff rule also covered no sleeping with staff. Damn it, he was a mess after Alana. More so than he feared if he was thinking even for a second of risking his family's reputation, and his own reputation as a worthy king, by sleeping with Kate. Nothing good would come from his moment of weakness, and then he'd be out an amazing assistant, because he couldn't allow her to work for him further. And she'd have a wealth of fodder for the press if she chose to turn against him.

That was precisely the reason he needed to keep his damn hands off his assistant.

"Maybe tomorrow we can rub it on each other, then," she suggested with a mocking grin. "Anyway, back to the charity."

Charity, the lesser of two evils when compared to rubbing sunscreen over her luscious curves... But he wasn't getting into this discussion again. He sponsored several organizations financially, but his time wasn't something he'd considered giving. The main reason being he didn't like it when people in power used that type of opportunity as just another publicity stunt. Luc didn't want to be that type of king...that is, if he actually got the crown.

"We need to figure out a plan to secure my title first," he told Kate. "Everything else can wait."

Pursing her lips, she nodded. Apparently, she was backing down, which was a first. She never shied away from an argument.

"You're plotting something," he said, narrowing his gaze. "You may as well tell me now."

"I'm not plotting anything," she replied, that sweet grin still in place, confirming his suspicion. "I've been thinking about your title, but I haven't come up with a solid solution, other than a quick wedding, of course."

She turned and started through the patio doors, but Luc reached out, grabbing her arm to halt her exit. Her eyes darted down to his hand, then back up to his face, but he didn't release her.

"Why is this particular charity so important to you?" he asked. "You mention it so often. If you give me the name, I'll send as much money as you want me to."

Her eyes softened, filled with a sadness he hadn't seen there before. "Money isn't what I wanted."

Slipping from his grasp, she headed down the stairs toward the beach. Money wasn't what she wanted? Had he ever heard a woman say that before? Surely any organization could benefit from a sizable donation.

Kate was always surprising him with what came out of her mouth. She seemed to enjoy a good verbal sparring as much as he did. But something about the cause she kept bringing up was bothering him. Obviously, this was something near and dear to her, and she didn't feel like opening up about it. She'd worked for him for a year, but he'd known her longer than that, though they didn't exactly hang in the same circles. Didn't she trust him enough to disclose her wishes?

Luc shook his head as he watched her walk along the

shoreline. The woman was mesmerizing from so many different angles, and it was a damn shame she was his assistant, because having her in his bed would certainly help take the edge off this title-throne nightmare.

Glancing up at the sky, he noticed the clouds growing darker. A storm was on the horizon and he knew how much Kate loved Mother Nature's wrath. She'd always been fascinated by the sheer power, she'd told him once. And that summed Kate up in a nutshell. She was fierce, moved with efficiency and had everyone taking notice.

Part of him wanted to worry, but he knew she'd be back soon, most likely to watch the storm from her own balcony. Luc still took a seat on his patio to wait for her, because they weren't done discussing this charity business. She was hiding something and he wanted to know what it was. Why was this mysterious organization such a secret? And why did discussing it make her so sad and closed off?

He sank down onto the cushioned bench beside the infinity pool. Everything about this outdoor living space was perfect and exactly what he would've chosen for himself. From the stone kitchen for entertaining to the wide, cushioned benches and chaise lounges by the pool, Luc loved all the richness this space offered.

Glancing down the beach where Kate had set out, he found he couldn't see her any longer and wondered when she'd start heading back. Ominous clouds blanketed the sky, rumbles of thunder filling the previous silence.

When the first fat drop of rain hit his cheek, Luc continued to stare in the direction she'd gone. Since when did he give anyone such power over his mind? He didn't like this. Not one bit.

He was next in line for the throne, for pity's sake.

How could his hormones be led around so easily by one petite, curvy woman, and how the hell could he still want her after months and months of ignoring the fact?

This pull was strong, no doubt, but Luc just had to be stronger. There was no room for lust here. He wouldn't risk his family's stellar reputation, or his ascension to the throne, just because he was hot for his assistant.

The wild, furious storm had been magnificent, one of the best she'd seen in a long time. Kate had meant to get back to the house before the weather got too bad, but she'd ended up finding a cove to wait it out in and couldn't resist staying outside. She'd been shielded from the elements, but she'd gotten drenched before she could get hunkered down.

With her dress plastered to her skin, she headed back toward the guesthouse. Even being soaking wet and a bit chilly from the breeze caressing her damp skin didn't dim her mood. She had to walk up the steps to Luc's patio in order to reach the path to her place. Noticing a light on the dock and lights on either side of the patio doors, she realized she'd been gone longer than she'd intended. It was clearly very dark and not because of the storm.

"Where the hell were you?"

Startled, Kate jumped back at the sound of Luc's angry, harsh tone. He stood in the doorway to his living area, wearing the same clothes as he had before, but now his hair stood on end, as if he'd run his fingers through it multiple times.

"Excuse me?" She stepped closer to him, taking in his flared nostrils, clenched jaw and the firm line of his mouth. "I told you I was going for a walk. I wasn't sure I had to check in, Dad."

Luc's lips thinned even more. "That storm was nasty. I assumed you'd have enough sense to come back. What the hell were you thinking?"

The fact he'd waited for her warmed something in her, but the way he looked as if he was ready to throttle her had her defensive side trumping all other feelings. This had nothing to do with lust or sexual chemistry.

"I purposely left the palace, the guards and everyone to get away from my troubles," he went on, his voice laced with irritation. "You're here to help me figure this whole mess out. But if you can't be responsible, you can either go back to the palace or I'll call in one of my guards to stay here and make sure you're safe."

Kate laughed. "You're being ridiculous. I'm a big girl, you know. I was perfectly fine and I sure as hell don't need a keeper. Next thing you know you'll be calling my parents."

With her father being head of security and her mother the clothing designer and seamstress for the family, Kate had been surrounded by royalty her entire life... just without a title of her own. Oh, wait, she was an assistant. Equally as glamorous as queen, princess or duchess.

Actually, she liked being behind the scenes. She had an important role that allowed her to travel, make great money and do some good without being in the limelight. And she would continue to try to persuade Luc to visit the orphanage so close to her heart. They'd taken care of her there, had loved her and sheltered her until she was adopted. Now she was in a position to return some of their generosity.

"Your father would agree with me." Luc stepped forward, closing the gap between them as he gripped her arm. "Don't go anywhere without your phone again. Anything could've happened to you."

"You can admit you were worried without going all Neanderthal on me, Your Highness." She jerked from his grasp, but he only stepped closer when she moved back. "What is your problem? I was out, I'm back. Don't be so grouchy because you can't admit you were scared."

"Scared?" he repeated, leaning in so close she could feel his warm breath on her face, see the gold flecks in those dark eyes. "I wasn't scared. I was angry that you were being negligent."

Kate really wasn't in the mood to be yelled at by her boss. She didn't deserve to be on the receiving end of his wrath when the issue he had was clearly with himself.

Her soggy dress needed to go, and she would give anything to soak in a hot bubble bath in that sunken garden tub in her master bathroom. She only hoped it worked. She hadn't tested it yet, and the sink in her kitchen was a bit leaky...

"I'm heading home." Kate waved a hand in the air to dismiss him and this absurd conversation. "We can talk tomorrow when you've cooled off."

The instant she turned away, she found herself being jerked back around. "I'm getting real sick of you manhandling—"

His lips were on hers, his hands gripping the sides of her face, holding her firmly in place as he coaxed her lips apart. There was nothing she could do but revel in the fact that Prince Lucas Silva was one potent man and quite possibly the best kisser she'd ever experienced.

And he was most definitely an experience. Those strong hands framed her face as his tongue danced with hers. Kate brought her hands up, wrapping them around his wrists. She had no clue if she should stop this before it got out of hand or hang on for the ride, since he'd fueled her every fantasy for so long.

Arching against him, she felt his firm body do so many glorious things to hers. The chill she'd had from the rain was no longer an issue.

But just as quickly as he'd claimed her mouth, he released her and stepped back, forcing her hands to drop. Muttering a Portuguese curse, Luc rubbed the back of his neck and kept his gaze on the ground. Kate honestly had no clue what to do. Say something? Walk away without a word?

What was the logical next step after being yelled at by her boss, then kissed as if he needed her like air in his lungs for his survival? And then pushed away with a filthy term her mother would blush at...

Clearing her throat, Kate wrapped her arms around her waist. "I'm not quite sure why you did that, but let's chalk it up to the heat of the moment. We'll both laugh about it tomorrow."

And dream about it tonight.

"You just push me too far." His intense gaze swept over her, but he kept his distance. "For a year I've argued with you, but you've always had my back. I know there've been times you've intervened and stood up for me without my even knowing. As far as employees go, you're the best."

Confused, Kate ran her hands up and down her arms as the ocean breeze chilled her damp skin. "Okay. Where are you going with this?"

"Nowhere," he all but yelled, flinging his arms out. "What just happened can't happen again because you're an employee and I don't sleep with staff. Ever."

Kate couldn't help the laugh that erupted from her. "You kissed me. Nobody mentioned sex."

His gaze heated her in ways that a hot bubble bath never could have. "I don't have to mention it. When I look at you I think it, and after tasting you, I feel it."

If he thought those words would deter her, he didn't know her at all. Kate reached forward, but Luc stepped back.

"Don't," he growled. "Just go on back to your cottage and we'll forget this happened."

Smoothing wet tendrils off her forehead, Kate shook her head. "Oh, no. You can't drop that bomb, give me a proverbial pat on the head and send me off to bed. You went from arguing to kissing me to throwing sex into the conversation in the span of two minutes. You'll understand if I can't keep up with your hormonal swings tonight."

The muscle tic in his jaw, the clenched fists at his sides, were all indicators he was irritated, frustrated and angry. He had no one to blame but himself, and she wasn't going to be caught up in his inner turmoil.

"This is ridiculous," she said with a sigh. "We're both obviously not in a position to talk without saying something we don't mean."

"I always mean what I say," he retorted. "Otherwise I wouldn't say it."

Rolling her eyes, Kate again waved a hand through the air. "Fine. You meant what you said about wanting to have sex with me."

"Don't twist my words," he growled.

Kate met his leveled gaze, knowing full well she was poking the bear. "Did you or did you not say you thought of having sex with me? That you actually feel it."

He moved around her, heading for the steps leading to the beach. "This conversation is over. Go home, Kate."

She stared at his retreating back for all of five seconds before she took off after him. Just because he was royalty and she was his assistant didn't mean he could dismiss her anytime he wanted. Rude was rude no matter one's social status.

She didn't say a word as she followed him. Luc's long strides ate up the ground as he headed toward the dock. Surely the man wasn't going out on his Jet Ski now. Granted, the water was calm since the storm had passed, but it was dark and he was angry.

Just as she was about to call his name, he went down. The heavy thud had her moving faster, her thighs burning from running across the sand. She prayed the sound of him falling was much worse than any injury.

"Luc," she called as she approached. "Are you all right?"

He didn't move, didn't respond, but lay perfectly still on the wet dock. Dread consumed her. The second she stepped onto the dock, her feet slid a bit, too, and she tripped over a loose board that had warped slightly higher than the others.

The dock obviously hadn't been repaired like the rest of the outdoor spaces on this property.

Kate crouched next to him, instantly noticing the swollen knot at his temple. He'd hit his head on a post, from what she could tell.

"Luc." She brushed his hair off his forehead, afraid to move him, and hoping he'd only passed out. "Can you hear me?"

She stroked his cheek as she ran her gaze down his body to see if there were any other injuries. How could he be up one second and out cold the next? Fear threatened to overtake her the instant she realized she didn't have her phone.

Maybe she was irresponsible, but she'd have to worry about that later. Right now she had no clue how serious Luc's injury was, but the fact he still hadn't moved had terror pumping through her.

Shifting so her knees weren't digging into the wood, Kate sat on her hip and kept patting Luc's face. "Come on, Luc. Wake up. Argue with me some more."

Torn between rushing back to the house for her phone to call for help and waiting to see if he woke on his own, Kate started patting down his shorts, hoping he carried his cell in his pocket.

One pocket was empty, and before she could reach to the other side, Luc groaned and tried to shift his body.

"Wait," she told him, pressing a hand to his shoulder as he started to rise. "Don't move. Are you hurt any-where?"

He blinked as he stared up at her. Thankfully, the bright light from the lamppost was helping her assess his injuries, since the sun had set.

Luc's brows drew together in confusion. "Why were you feeling me up?"

Relief swept through her. "I wasn't feeling you up," she retorted, wrapping her arm around his shoulders and slowly helping him to sit up. "I was checking your pockets for a cell phone. You fell and hit your head on the post. I was worried because you were out for a few minutes."

Luc reached up, wincing as his fingers encountered the bump on his head, which was already turning blue. "Damn, that hurts."

"Let's get you back up to the house." Kate helped

him to his feet, then slid her arm around his waist to steady him. "You okay? Feeling dizzy or anything?"

He stared down at her, blinked a few times and frowned. "This is crazy," he muttered.

"What?"

With his thumb and index finger, he wiped his eyes and held the bridge of his nose. He probably had the mother of all headaches right now. All the more reason to get this big guy moving toward the house, because if he went back down, she couldn't carry him.

"I know you," he murmured. "I just... Damn it, your name isn't coming to me."

Kate froze. "You don't know my name?" This was not good. That ball of fear in her stomach grew.

Shaking his head, he wrapped an arm around her shoulders and started leading them off the dock. "I must've hit my head harder than I thought. Why isn't it coming to me?"

Kate pressed a hand to his abdomen, halting his progress. She shifted just enough to look him in the eyes. Since she wasn't a medic and never had any kind of training other than a basic CPR course, she had no idea what signs to look for with a head trauma.

"Look at me," she ordered. "You know me, Luc. You know my name."

Blowing out a breath, he hung his head. "I... It's on the tip of my tongue. Damn, why can't I remember?"

He glanced back up at her, worry filling his dark eyes. This was not good, not good at all. She was going to have to get him back to the house and call the palace doctor. Obviously, Luc's memory wasn't cooperating. But she didn't want him panicking; she could do enough of that for both of them.

"My name is Kate." She watched his eyes, hoping

to see some recognition, but there was nothing. "I'm your—"

"Fiancée." A wide smile spread across his face. "Now I remember you."

Luc leaned in to capture her lips once more, with a passion she'd never known.

Three

Fiancée? What the hell?

Mustering all her willpower, Kate pushed Luc and his intoxicating mouth away as his words slammed into her.

"Let's get you inside," she told him, trying not to focus on how hard he must've hit his head, because he was clearly not in his right mind. "I'm not comfortable with that knot you have, and you may have a concussion. I need to call your doctor. Hopefully, with the storm gone, we'll have cell service."

Luc stared at her another minute, then nodded. Slipping his arm around her shoulders again, he let her lead him up to the house. Something was definitely wrong with him. The Luc from only twenty minutes ago would be arguing that he didn't need a doctor, and he certainly wouldn't be leaning on her for support.

She couldn't even think about the fact that he believed they were engaged. Because if he thought they were sleeping together, this situation would get extremely awkward really fast.

Though she'd be lying if she didn't admit to herself just how much she liked him thinking they were a couple. How long would his mind play this trick on him? How would he treat her now that he believed they were together?

Once she had him inside and settled on the sofa, she stood up and caught her breath. Luc was one massive, thick, muscular man. She'd known he was cut, but she'd had no clue how solid and heavy he would be.

His body had leaned against hers, twisting her dress on their walk. As Kate readjusted herself, trying to refill her lungs with air and not panic, she found him staring up at her, that darkened gaze holding her in place. Shivers rippled through her at the intensity of the moment—and the man.

"What?" she asked.

"Why are you all wet?"

Plucking at the damp material that clung to her thighs, Kate shook her head. "I got caught outside in the storm earlier."

Those eyes continued to rake over her body. "You're sexy like this," he murmured as his heated stare traveled back up. "With your dress clinging to your curves and your hair messy and wavy."

Kate swallowed, because any reply she had to those intimate words would lead to a lie, and she couldn't let him keep thinking they were anything more than employee-employer, servant-royal.

"Where's your cell?" If she didn't stay on task, she'd get caught up in all those sultry looks he was giving her...and she desperately wanted to get caught up in the promise behind those sexy stares. But he wasn't himself right now. "I need to call the doctor. I hope we have service."

Luc glanced around, raking a hand through his hair. "I have no idea. I don't even remember why I was outside."

He slapped his hand on the cushion beside him and let out a string of curses. "Why can't I remember anything?"

The worry lacing his voice concerned her even more than the fact he thought they were engaged. Luc Silva never let his guard down. Even when faced with losing the crown, the man was the epitome of control and power. Sexy and strong and she wanted him. Plain and simple…or maybe not so simple considering she could never have him.

"It's okay," she assured him as she leaned down to pat his shoulder. "I'll find it. Once the doctor comes, we'll know more. Maybe this will only last a few minutes. Try not to panic."

That last bit of advice was for herself as much as him, because she was seriously in panic mode right now. She didn't know much about memory loss, but the fact that something had set his mind so off balance concerned her. She couldn't even imagine how he felt.

Kate walked around the spacious but sparsely decorated living room, into the dated kitchen and then back to the living room. Crossing to the patio doors they'd just entered, she finally spotted his cell lying on the old, worn accent table most likely left by the last tenants.

Thankfully, she knew the passcode to get into the phone. "I'm just going to step out here," she told him, trying to assure him he wouldn't be alone. "I'll be right back."

She didn't want Luc to hear any worry in her tone when she described the incident to the doctor. And for now, she wasn't going to mention the whole "fiancée" bit. She would ride this out as long as possible. Yes, that was selfish, but, well…everyone had their moments of weakness and Luc Silva was definitely her weakness.

Kate was relieved to get the doctor on the phone and even more relieved when he promised to be there within the next hour. For the next sixty minutes, Luc would most likely believe they were engaged and she would play right along until she was told otherwise.

Luc's private beach villa just off the coast of Portugal wasn't far from his own country. He was pretty much hiding in plain sight. This way he could be home quickly in an emergency—or someone could come to him.

Kate was grateful the doctor could use the private boat to get to the island. There was no airstrip and the only way in or out was via boat. Only yesterday she and Luc had been dropped off by her father, so Luc could keep his hideout a secret.

When she walked back inside, Luc had his head tipped back against the sofa cushions. Eyes closed, he held a hand to his head, massaging his temples with his fingers.

"The doctor is on his way."

Without opening his eyes, he simply gave a brief nod.

"I know you're hurting, but I don't want to give you anything before the doctor can examine you."

What if his injuries were more serious than she thought? Amnesia, temporary or not, wasn't the worst thing that could happen. People died from simple falls all the time. Even when they felt fine, they could have some underlying issue that went unnoticed.

The possibilities flooded her mind as she continued to stand across the room and stare at Luc. Should he be resting or should she keep him awake? She prayed she didn't do the wrong thing. She would never forgive herself if something happened to him because they'd been fighting and he'd stormed off. If she didn't always feel the need to challenge him, this wouldn't have happened.

The kiss wouldn't have happened, either, because that was obviously spawned from sexual frustration and anger. Luc's full-on mouth attack had been forceful, not gentle or restrained. She'd loved every delicious second of it. But now she needed to focus, not think about how good it had felt to finally have him touch her the way she'd always wanted.

As she watched him, his lids kept fluttering, and finally remained closed for a minute.

"Luc," she said softly. "Try not to fall asleep, okay?"

"I'm not," he mumbled. "The lights are too bright, so I'm just keeping my eyes closed."

Crossing to the switches, she killed the lights in the living room, leaving just the one from the kitchen on so she could still see him.

"Does that help?" she asked, taking a seat beside him on the couch, relishing in the warmth from his body.

He opened one eye, then the other, before he shifted slightly to look at her. "Yeah. Thanks."

When he reached over to take her hand, Kate tensed. This wasn't real. The comfort he was seeking from her was only because he was uncertain—and he thought they were engaged.

Oh, if they were truly engaged, Kate could hold his hand and not feel guilty. She could wrap her arms around him and give him support and love and…

But no. She wasn't his fianceé so thinking along those lines would get her nowhere.

For now, she could pretend, she could keep her fingers laced with his and feel things for him in ways she never had before. This was no longer professional... they'd crossed that threshold when he'd captured her mouth beneath his.

"I'll be fine." Luc offered a wide smile, one rarely directed at her. "Just stay right here with me."

Swallowing the truth, Kate nodded. "I'm not going anywhere."

She tried not to relish the fact that Luc's thumb kept stroking the back of her hand. She tried to fight the thrill that he was looking at her as more than just an employee.

None of this was reality. He was trapped in his own mind for now. She didn't know if she should focus on the kiss earlier or the nasty knot on his head. Both issues made her a nervous wreck.

The hour seemed to crawl by, but when Dr. Couchot finally knocked on the back door, Kate breathed a sigh of relief. Beneath her hand, Luc tensed.

"It's okay." She rose to her feet, patting his leg. "We'll figure this out and you'll be just fine."

Dr. Couchot immediately came inside, set his bag down and took a seat on the couch next to Luc.

"Tell me what happened," he said, looking at Kate. Worry was etched on the doctor's face. This man had cared for Luc since the prince had been in diapers, and held all the royals' medical secrets.

Kate recounted the events, omitting the fiancée bit, and watched as the doctor examined his patient while she spoke. He looked at Luc's pupils with his minuscule light, then lightly worked his fingertip around the blue knot. With a frown, he sat back and sighed.

"Have you remembered anything since I was called?" he asked.

Luc shook his head. "I know Kate, but she had to tell me her name. I know I'm a member of the royal family because of my name, and I believe I'm the prince. I know this house is mine and I know I wanted to fix it up, but apparently I didn't get too far, so I had to have just bought it."

All this was right. A little burst of hope spread through Kate. Maybe his injuries weren't as bad as she'd first feared.

"From what I can tell, you've got temporary amnesia," the doctor stated. "I'm not seeing signs of a concussion and your pupils are responsive." Dr. Couchot looked up at Kate. "I would like him to have a scan to be on the safe side, but knowing Luc, he'll be stubborn and refuse."

"I'm sitting right here," Luc stated, his eyes darting between Kate and the doctor. "I don't want to get a scan. I'd have to go home and face too many questions. Unless I'm at risk for something more serious, I'm staying here."

Kate shared a look with the doctor. "What about if I promise to monitor him? You said there was no concussion, so that's a good sign."

"Fine," Dr. Couchot conceded. "I won't argue. But Kate will have her eyes on you 24/7 for the next few days and I'll be in contact with her. At the first sign of anything unusual, she will get you back to the palace, where we can treat you. No exceptions."

Luc nodded. "Agreed."

After receiving her instructions and a list of things

to look for in terms of Luc's behavior, Kate showed the doctor out.

Once they reached the edge of the patio, Dr. Couchot turned to face her. "Make sure you don't force any memories on him. It's important he remembers on his own, or his mind could become even more confused and his condition could actually worsen. It's a blessing he remembers as much as he does, so I believe he's only lost a few months of his memories."

A few months. Which would explain why he didn't recall the real fiancée or the fake pregnancy.

"I'll make sure not to feed him any information," Kate promised. Smoothing her hair back, she held it to the side in a makeshift ponytail. "Can he see photos or listen to his favorite music? Maybe just subtle things that will spark his thoughts?"

"I think that would be fine. Just don't push all of that on him at once. Give this some time. He may wake tomorrow and be perfectly fine, or he may be like this for another month. Every mind is unique, so we just don't know."

Kate nodded, thanking the doctor for coming so quickly. She watched as he made his way back down to the boat, where a palace guard was waiting. Thankfully, it wasn't her father, but his right-hand man.

Kate gave a wave to the men and took in a deep breath. When the doctor mentioned unusual behavior, did that include believing you were engaged to the wrong woman?

Weary and worried, she stepped back through the doors. All her stuff was at the guesthouse, but she would need to stay here.

Luc's eyes were instantly on hers when she returned to the living room. That warmth spread through her once again as she recognized that look of need. She couldn't let him keep this up. There would be no way she could resist him. And based on his reaction after that kiss, he wouldn't be happy that he'd indulged his desire for her, no matter how good together they might be.

The warning from the doctor played over in her mind. She couldn't force memories, so for now she'd have to let him think what he wanted, until his mind started to cooperate.

"Sit with me," he whispered, holding his hand out in invitation.

Kate cringed, wanting nothing more than to take his hand and settle in beside him. "I need to go get some of my things."

Lowering his hand, he frowned. "Where are your things?"

Coming up with a quick excuse, she tried to be vague, yet as honest as possible. "I have some things next door at the guesthouse. Let me get them and I'll be all yours."

Okay, she didn't necessarily need to add that last bit, but it just slipped out. She'd have to think through every single word until Luc fully regained his memory. For now, she'd have to play along...and still try to maintain some distance, or she could find herself in a world of hurt when he snapped out of his current state. Getting wrapped up in this make-believe world, even for a short time, wasn't the wisest decision. Still, he would need her during this time and they were on this island together. How could she resist him? How could she resist more touching, more kissing?

"Why do you have anything next door?" he asked.

"I was working there earlier." Still not a lie. "Give me five minutes. I'll be right back."

She escaped out the back door, unable to look at the confusion on his face any longer. If she got too far into the truth as to why she had things at the cottage, she'd have to come clean and produce the information his mind wasn't ready for.

As quickly as she could, she threw a change of clothes into her bag, adding a few essential toiletries. Everything else she'd have to smuggle over a little at a time, provided she stayed at the main house for longer than a few days.

Her biggest concern now was the fact she hadn't packed pajamas, assuming she'd be living alone. She stared at her pile of silky chemises in various colors. There was no getting around this. She didn't even have an old T-shirt to throw on for a sleep shirt.

With no other choice, she grabbed the pink one and shoved it in her bag before heading back to the main house. There was no way she could let Luc see her in this chemise, but how could she dodge a man who thought they were engaged? Most likely he assumed they slept together, too.

Kate froze on the path back to the main house. There was no way she could sleep with Luc. None. If they shared the same bed, she'd be tempted to give in to his advances.

As the moonlight lit her way back, Kate was resigned to the fact that things were about to skyrocket to a whole new level of awkward.

Four

Kate glanced over her shoulder, making sure she was alone as she slipped back out onto the patio to call her mother. There were times in a woman's life she just needed some motherly advice, and for Kate, that time was now.

"Darling!" Her mother answered on the second ring. "I was just thinking of you."

"Hey, Mama." Kate leaned against the rail on the edge of the patio, facing the doorway to make sure Luc didn't come up behind her and overhear things he shouldn't. "Are you busy?"

"Never for you. You sound funny. Everything all right?"

Not even close. Kate sighed, shoving her hair behind her ear. "I'm in a bit of a bind and I need your advice."

"What's wrong, Katelyn?"

Her mother's worried tone slid through the line. Kate swallowed back her emotions, because tears wouldn't fix this problem and they would only get her a snotty nose and red eyes. Not a good look when one was shacking up with one's sexy boss.

"Luc fell earlier."

"Oh, honey. Is he okay?"

"Well…he has a good-sized goose egg on his head. And he has temporary amnesia."

"Amnesia?" her mother repeated, her voice rising an octave. "Katelyn, are you guys coming back to the palace? Do his parents know?"

"I actually called them before I called you. Dr. Couchot was just here and he's assured us that Luc is okay, no concussion or anything. He isn't sure when Luc will regain his memory, but he's confident it's a short-term condition."

"I can't even imagine how scary this must be," her mother commented. "What can I do to help?"

"Right now Luc and I are staying here as planned," Kate stated, her eyes darting to the patio doors on the far side of the house. Luc stood there for a moment, looking out at the ocean, before he turned and disappeared. "The doctor said keeping him relaxed and calm is best for now. Luc had wanted to get away, so staying here is still our best option."

"I agree. So what else has you upset? If the doctor has assured you this is temporary, and you're staying there as planned, what's wrong?"

Pulling in a deep breath, Kate blurted out, "He thinks we're engaged."

Silence settled over the line. Kate pulled her cell away from her ear to make sure the connection hadn't been cut.

"Mom?"

"I'm here. I just need to process this," her mother stated. "Why does he think you're engaged?"

"He's only lost the past few months. He knew I was familiar, but at first he couldn't place me. When I told him my name, he assumed we were engaged. I was worried and didn't say anything, because I wanted the doctor to look him over. Dr. Couchot said not to feed Luc any information, because giving him pieces of his recent past could mess up his memory even further."

Kate rambled on. She knew she was talking fast, but she needed to get all this out, needed to get advice with Luc out of earshot.

"The doctor and Luc's parents have no clue that Luc believes we're engaged," Kate went on. "That's what I need your opinion on. What do I do, Mom? I don't want to go against the doctor's orders, but at the same time, I can't have him thinking we're a couple, but he doesn't even recall I work for him. You know how this family feels about dating or having such personal relationships with their staff."

"Oh, Katelyn." Her mother sighed. "I would wait and see how tonight goes. If this is temporary, maybe Luc will wake up tomorrow and everything will be fine. You can't go against the doctor's wishes, but I wouldn't let this lie go on too long. Luc may cross boundaries that you two shouldn't cross if he thinks you're his fiancée."

Cross boundaries? Too late. The kiss they'd shared moments before his fall flashed through her mind.

"Thanks, Mom. Please don't say anything. You're the only one who knows Luc thinks we're getting married. I don't want to humiliate him any further or have anyone else worry. I just needed your advice."

"I'm not sure I helped, but I'm definitely here for you. Please, keep me posted. I worry about you."

Kate smiled, pushing herself off the railing and heading back toward the doors. "I know. I'll call you tomorrow if the cell service is good. It's pretty sketchy here."

"Love you, sweetheart."

"I love you, Mama."

Kate disconnected the call as she grasped the doorknob. Closing her eyes, she pulled in a deep breath and blew it out slowly. She needed strength, wisdom and more self-control than ever.

And she needed to remember that Luc was healing. That he was confused. Whatever emotions she'd held on to after that kiss had no place here. Being this close to grasp onto her fantasy, yet not being allowed to take all she wanted was a level of agony she hadn't even known existed.

Luc stood in the spacious bedroom. Apparently, his master suite and luxurious attached bath, with a most impressive shower that gave the illusion of being outdoors, had been at the top of his list for renovations. Fine with him, because this room was fit for romance, and his Kate had looked all sorts of sexy the way she'd worried over him, assuring him he would be okay.

When she'd said it, her sweet, yet confident words had sliced through the fear he'd accumulated. He'd seen the worry in her eyes, but she'd put up a strong front for him. Was it any wonder she was the one for him? Dread over the unknown kept creeping up, threatening to consume him, but Luc wasn't giving up. Being unable to recall bits of his life was beyond weird and frustrating. He actually didn't have the words to describe the emotions flooding him. All he knew was that his beautiful fiancée was here, and she was staying by his side, offering support and comfort.

His eyes drifted from his reflection in the glass patio doors back to the king-size bed dominating the middle of the room. Sheers draping down from the ceiling enclosed the bed, giving an impression of romance and seduction. There was a reason this bed was the focal point of the room, and he had to assume it all centered around Kate. He could already picture her laid out on those satin navy sheets, her black hair fanned out as they made love.

Damn it. Why couldn't he remember making love to her? Why couldn't he recall how she felt against him? How she tasted when he kissed her? Maybe their intimacy would help awaken some of those memories.

Luc cringed inwardly. No, he wasn't using sex or Kate in that way. He wanted to remember their love on his own, but he definitely wanted her by his side tonight while he slept. He wanted to hold her next to him, to curl around her and lose himself to dreams. Maybe tomorrow he'd wake and all this would be a nightmare. His memory would be back and he and Kate could move forward.

There had to be something lying around, some clue that would spark his memory. Granted, he hadn't really brought anything personal to the place, judging by the hideously dated furniture in the majority of the rooms, but surely there was something. Even if he looked through the clothes he'd brought, or maybe there was something in his wallet that would kick his mind back into the proper gear. Perhaps he'd packed something personal, like a picture, or maybe he should go through the contacts on his cell. Seeing a list of names might be just the trigger he needed.

Luc searched through his drawers, finding nothing of interest. It wasn't as if his underwear drawer would reveal any hidden clues other than the fact that he liked black boxer briefs.

Slamming one drawer shut, he searched another. By the time he was done looking through the chest and hunting through his bathroom, he was alternating between being terrified and being furious. Nothing new popped up except a healthy dose of rage.

There had to be something in his cell phone. He started out the bedroom door, only to collide chest to chest with Kate. Her eyes widened as she gripped his biceps in an attempt to steady herself.

"Sorry," she said, stepping back. "I just got back with my things. I called your parents and gave them the rundown. They're worried, but I assured them you would be fine and you'd call them yourself tomorrow. I also called my mother. I didn't mean to be gone so long. Are you heading to bed?"

Was she shaking? Her eyes darted over his shoulder toward the bed, then back to meet his gaze. The fact she had been rambling and now kept chewing on her lip was proof she was nervous. About the amnesia?

"Are you all right?" he asked, reaching out to smooth her hair away from her forehead. He tipped her chin up, focusing on those luscious, unpainted lips. "You seem scared, more than you were just a few minutes ago."

Kate reached up to take his hand in hers. "I guess all the events finally caught up with me. I'm tired and worried. Nothing more."

"That's more than you need to handle," he told her, stroking his thumb over her bottom lip. "Let's go to bed."

That instant, holding Kate completely trumped finding his phone and seeking answers. There was a need inside him, an ache he had for this woman that was so primal he couldn't even wrap his mind around it. His phone would be there when he woke up, and right now all he wanted was to lose himself in Kate. She looked dead on her feet, and she still hadn't changed from her wet dress, which had now mostly dried. There was no way she was comfortable.

"Why don't you grab a shower and meet me in bed?" he asked.

Her eyes widened. "Um…I'm not sure we should…"

Luc waited for her to elaborate, but she closed her eyes and let out a soft sigh. When her head drooped a little, Luc dropped his hand from her chin and squeezed her shoulder.

"Are you afraid to be with me because of the memory loss?"

Her lids lifted, her dark eyes searching his. "I'm not afraid of you, Luc. I think it would be best if we didn't… you know…"

"Make love?"

A pink tinge crept across her tan cheeks. "Yes. You're injured. You need to rest and relax. Per the doctor's orders."

Luc snaked his arms around her waist as he pulled her flush against his body. "I plan on relaxing, but I want you lying beside me. It's obvious we came here to get away, and I don't want to ruin this trip for you."

Delicate hands slid up his chest, fingers curling up over his shoulders. Just her simple touch was enough to have his body quivering, aching. Everything about her was so familiar, yet so new at the same time.

"You're not ruining anything for me." She offered a tired, yet beautiful smile. "Let's just concentrate on getting you better, and everything else will fall into place."

"So no sex, but you'll lie down with me?"

Her eyes held his as she nodded. "I'll lie with you."

He hadn't recalled her name at first, but he'd instantly felt a pull toward her. No wonder they were engaged. Obviously, they shared a special, deeply rooted bond. Their chemistry pushed through the damage to his mind, and that alone would help him pull through this.

"I'll just go shower in the guest bath, real quick," she told him, easing away from his embrace. "Give me ten minutes."

Confused at her need to retreat, Luc crossed his arms over his chest. "Why not just use the shower in here? The other bathroom hasn't been renovated and this one is much more luxurious."

She looked as if she wanted to argue, but finally nodded. "You're right. A quick shower in here would be better. I just didn't know if I would disturb you trying to rest."

"You won't bother me. You can take advantage of the sunken garden tub, you know." He took her hands, leading her farther into their bedroom. "No need to rush through a shower. Just go soak in a tubful of warm water and relax."

"I'll be quick in the shower. Why don't you lie down?"

He leaned forward, gently touching his lips to hers. "Don't take too long or I'll come in after you."

She shivered beneath his touch, and it was all Luc could do to keep from hauling her off to the bed and taking what he wanted, throwing every reason he shouldn't straight out the window.

Retreating into the bathroom, she closed the door. Luc frowned. Was she always so private? Why did some things seem so familiar, while other, mundane things had disappeared from his mind?

As he stripped down to his boxer briefs, he heard the

shower running. An image of a wet, soapy Kate flooded his mind. He couldn't wait to get beyond this memory lapse, beyond the annoyance of the headache, and make full use of that spacious shower with her.

He would make this up to her, somehow. His Kate was exhausted, and still worried about him. She was sacrificing, when this was supposed to be a romantic trip away.

As of right now he only remembered they were engaged. He recalled some buzz about wedding invitations and upcoming showers. He'd let his assistant handle all of that…but he couldn't recall who his assistant was at the moment.

Raking a hand down his face, Luc sighed. Now wasn't the time to think of staff, not when he was about to crawl into bed with his fianceé. Right now he wanted to focus on Kate, on their trip and somehow making this up to her.

Kate showered quickly, constantly watching the door she'd closed. She should've known he'd want her in his room, that he wouldn't even question the fact.

But sleeping with him under false pretenses was an absolute no.

No matter how Luc made her body tingle and the nerves in her belly dance…she couldn't let her thoughts go there.

She was still Luc's assistant, which meant looking out for his best interest. And it was in the interest of both of them to keep their clothes on. Easier said than done.

Kate dried off, wrapped her hair up in a towel and slid into her chemise. She truly had no other option unless she asked Luc for a T-shirt, but she didn't know if he was one of those guys who would be even more turned on by seeing a woman in his clothes, so she opted for her own gown.

Rubbing the towel through her wet hair, she got all the moisture out and took her time brushing it. Perhaps if she stayed away a few extra minutes, Luc would get tired and fall asleep before she went back out there.

Their argument before his fall had taken on a life of its own, and she still couldn't get that kiss from her mind. Of course, if her lips weren't still tingling, maybe she could focus on something else. Such as the fact that the man was suffering from memory loss and was scared and angry over this sudden lack of control with his own mind.

Still, between the toe-curling kiss and the fact she was about to slide between the sheets with her boss, Kate didn't know how to act at this point. What was the proper protocol?

After applying some lotion on her legs and shoulders, Kate hung up her towel and faced the inevitable: she was going to have to go out into the bedroom and get in that bed. The sooner she moved beyond the awkward, uncomfortable stage, the sooner she could breathe easily. All she needed to do was go in there, lie beside Luc and wait for him to fall asleep. Then she could get up and go to the sofa or something. No way could she lie nestled next to him all night. The temptation to pick up where their kiss had left off would be too strong.

But the doctor had been adamant about not saying too much, to allow the memories to return on their own. Kate didn't want to do anything that would cause Luc more damage.

Somehow she had to abide by his no-fraternization

rule and still manage to play the doting fiancée. Was that combination even possible?

Taking a deep breath, she opened the bathroom door. The darkened room was a welcome sight. At least this way she wouldn't have to look him in the eye and lie. Now the only light spilled from the bathroom, slashing directly across the bed in the center of the room as if putting all the focus on Luc and his bare chest. The covers were up to his waist; his arms were crossed and resting on his forehead.

"Turn off the light and get in bed."

The memory loss didn't affect his commanding ways. The man demanded, he never asked, and he expected people to obey. Still, the low, powerful tone he used was enough to have her toes curling on the hardwood. This was her fantasy come to life, though when she'd envisioned Luc ordering her into bed, she never imagined quite this scenario.

What a way for fate to really stick it to her and mock her every dream with this false one.

"Is your head still hurting?" she asked, remaining in the bathroom doorway.

"It's a dull pain, but better than it was."

Kate tapped the switch, sending the room into darkness, save for the soft moonlight sweeping through the balcony doors. The pale tile floor combined with the moon was enough to light her path to the bed.

Pulling the covers back, she eased down as gently as possible and lay on her back. On the edge. As stiff as a board. And the ache for him only grew as his masculine scent surrounded her and his body heat warmed the minuscule space between them.

The bed dipped as Luc rolled toward her. "Are you okay?"

His body fitted perfectly against hers. Just the brush of the coarse hair on his legs against her smooth ones had her senses on alert...as if they needed to be heightened.

Was she okay? Not really. On one hand she was terrified. On the other she was completely intrigued...and spiraling headfirst into arousal. And arousal was taking the lead over so many emotions. With his breath tickling her skin, she was fully consumed by the one man she'd wanted for so long. It would be so easy, yet so wrong, to roll over and take what she wanted.

"I'm fine," she assured him.

With the darkness surrounding them, the intimacy level seemed to soar. She should've insisted on a small light or something. But then she would see his face. Honestly, she had no clue what was more torturous.

"You're tense."

Understatement of the year.

Luc's hand trailed up her arm, moving to rest on her stomach. If he thought she was tense before, he should just keep touching her. She was about to turn to stone.

She needed to regain control of her body, her hormones. Unfortunately, her mind and her girlie parts were not corresponding very well right now, because she was getting hot, restless, as if she needed to shift toward him for more of that delicate touching he was offering.

No. This was wrong. Her even thinking of wanting more was wrong. Just because he'd kissed her earlier didn't mean a thing. He'd done so to shut her up, to prove a point and to take charge as he always did.

Yet given the way he'd masterfully taken over and kissed her with such force and passion, there was no way he'd been unmoved. And she would've called him on it, but now she was dealing with a new set of issues surrounding her desires.

"If you're worried about me, I'm fine," he assured her. "I just want to lie here and hold you. Scoot over against me. I feel like you're about ready to fall out of the bed."

Just as she started to shift, her knee brushed against him. His unmistakable arousal had her stopping short.

"Ignore it," he said with a laugh. "I'm trying like hell."

Squeezing her eyes shut, Kate sighed. "I can't do this."

Five

Luc grabbed Kate around the waist just as she started to get up. Pulling her flush against him, her back against his chest, he held on tight. Her silky gown slid over his bare chest, adding fuel to the already out-of-control fire.

"Don't," he whispered in her ear, clutching the silk material around her stomach, keeping her body taut against his own. "Just relax."

"You need to be sleeping."

Her body was still so stiff, so rigid beneath him. Something had seriously freaked her out and she wasn't telling him what it was. Damn it, was it something he already knew but couldn't recall? Or was this not about her at all, but something to do with his fall?

A sliver of fear slid through him.

"Did the doctor say something you're not telling me?" he asked.

"What? No."

She shifted, relaxing just a touch as she laid her hand over his on her stomach. The first contact she'd initiated since climbing into bed.

"He didn't say much when I walked him out," she went on. "Just that he felt it necessary for you to remember on your own."

"The only thing I want to do right now is to get you to relax."

Luc slid his hand out from beneath hers, to the lacy edge of her silk gown. Her body stiffened briefly, then arched as if she was fighting her own arousal. When she sucked in a breath, Luc knew he had her.

"Luc, you need to rest."

Her shaky voice betrayed her, indicating she was just as achy and excited as he was. He pushed one of her legs back, easing his fingers beneath the silk until he found the delicate elastic edge on her panties.

"What I need to do is pleasure my woman," he whispered in her ear, pleased when she trembled.

Kate's back arched again and her head fell against his shoulder. "Luc, you don't have to—"

He nipped at the tender flesh of her earlobe as he eased his hand inside her panties to stroke her. "I want to."

Her soft moans, her cry when he found just the right spot, left his mouth dry. It didn't take long for her body to give in and shudder beneath his touch. She gasped, trembled all the while Luc trailed kisses along her shoulder, her neck when she'd turn just so and the soft spot below her ear.

Yet nothing triggered any memories.

All the same, he didn't regret giving her pleasure. Everything about this private moment only made him want her, yearn for her more.

"Are you always this responsive?" he whispered.

Slowly, she rolled toward him, rested a palm on his chest. With the pale glow from the moon, he didn't miss the shimmer in Kate's eyes.

"Baby, don't cry."

She blinked, causing more tears to slide down her flushed cheeks. "You didn't remember, though, did you?"

He smoothed her damp hair away from her face. "No."

When her hand started down his abdomen, toward the top of his boxer briefs, he gripped her wrist.

Kate had been through a rough time, and even though he was the one suffering the medical concern, he wasn't about to let her think he'd given her pleasure only to get his own. This moment was all about her, reassuring her that he—no, that they—would be okay.

"We both need to rest right now," he told her, dropping a kiss to her forehead. "You're exhausted, I'm recovering. We'll make love tomorrow and I'll make this up to you, Kate. Our trip won't be ruined. I promise."

So stupid. Foolish, careless and flat-out irresponsible.

First she'd let him touch her, then she'd cried. The tears came instantly after she'd crashed back into reality after the most amazing climax she'd ever had.

The moment had been so consuming, so mind-blowing. That's when she knew Luc hadn't remembered anything, or he would've been angry to be in that position with her.

So when the tears fell, she'd had no way to stop them.

What should've been a beautiful moment was tarnished by the situation. She hadn't expected Luc to be so powerful in bed. She truly had no idea how she'd hold him off from becoming intimate now that they'd shared such passion.

Kate had eased from the bed early this morning. Her vow to leave and sleep on the couch as soon as he fell asleep had gone out the window. After his mission to relax her had been a success, she'd been dead to the world.

How had this bizarre scenario spiraled so far out of control? She'd just spent the night in her boss's arms, a boss who was a prince, a boss who thought she was his fiancée. He was a man who prided himself on control and keeping his professional and personal lives separate. The rule was very clear at the palace.

Everything that had happened in the past eighteen hours was a colossal mess.

Kate had hurried back to her cottage early this morning while Luc slept. She'd managed to smuggle a couple sundresses and her swimsuit over. That should get her through the next few days, though she prayed she wouldn't be here that long.

Her cell phone vibrated in the pocket of her short dress. Pulling it out, she was thankful the service seemed to be holding up. The doctor's name lit up her screen.

"Good morning, Dr. Couchot," she said, as if she hadn't had the most life-altering night she'd ever experienced.

"Kate, how is Luc this morning?"

Glancing over her shoulder toward the open patio doors, she saw him still sprawled out on the bed, asleep. She kept checking on him, but he'd grumble and roll back over. She had to assume he was fine, since he was resting so well.

"He's sleeping in today," she told the doctor, turning back to watch the gentle waves ebb and flow against the shoreline. "He was exhausted last night."

"I imagine so. Still nothing new to report? No change in the memory or new symptoms?"

Kate leaned against the wrought-iron railing and wondered if the toe-curling intimacy was worth reporting. Probably best to leave that out of the conversation.

"No. He's the same."

The same sexy, determined, controlling man he always was, just with a sweeter side he was willing to share. And he was oh so giving between the sheets...

Dr. Couchot reiterated how Kate was to just let Luc think on his own, let the memories return as slowly or as fast as his mind needed them to. As if she needed reminding. Nearly all she could focus on was keeping this colossal secret.

Once she hung up, she turned, leaning her back against the rail. Watching him sleep was probably wrong, too, but why stop now? She hadn't done anything right since she'd gotten here. In the span of three days she'd fought with him, kissed him, come undone in his bed and played the part of the doting fiancée. How could she make things any worse?

Kate just prayed he'd get his memory back so they could move on. The lies were eating at her and she didn't know how she could keep up this charade.

Luc was a fighter in every way. He wouldn't let this memory loss keep him down. He'd claw his way back up from the abyss and then...

Yeah, that was the ultimate question. And then... what? Would he hate her? Would he fire her? Would he look at her with disdain?

A sick pit formed in the depths of her stomach. Would her parents lose their jobs? Surely her mom and dad would be disappointed in her for breaking the royal protocol.

This couldn't go on. Luc had to remember. So far she hadn't given Luc any extra information regarding his past, and she didn't intend to because she didn't want to make his issue worse. But there was only so long she could go on not telling him things. The man wanted to sleep with her.

How did she keep dodging that fact when she wanted it, too?

The way he'd looked at her, with affection, was so new and so tempting. And all built on lies.

Luc called out in his sleep. Kate straightened as she slowly moved closer. When he cried out again, she still couldn't make out what he was saying. She set her phone on the nightstand and eased down on the edge of the bed. His bronze chest stared back at her and Kate had a hard time not touching him, not running her finger-tips over the tip of the tattoo that slid perfectly over one shoulder.

The sheet had dipped low, low enough to show one hip and just the edge of his black boxer briefs. She'd felt those briefs against her skin last night. More impres-sively, she'd felt what was beneath them.

"Tell me," he muttered, shifting once again. His eyes were squeezed tight, as if he was trying to fight what-ever image had him twisting in the sheets.

Kate froze. Was he remembering something? Would his memory come back and play through his mind like a movie?

When his face scrunched even more and his chin started quivering, she knew he was fighting some demon, and she couldn't just sit here and watch him suffer. She might not be able to fully disclose the truth, but she didn't have to witness the man's complete down-fall, either.

"Luc." She placed her hand on his shoulder and shook him gently. "Luc."

Jerking awake, he stared up at her, blinking a few times as if to get his bearings. Kate pulled her hand back, needing to keep her touching at a minimum.

Raking a hand down his face, his day-old stubble rustling beneath his palm, he let out a sigh. "That was insane. I was dreaming about a baby," he murmured, his gaze dipping to her midsection. "Are we having a baby, Kate?"

On this she could be absolutely honest. For once.

"No, we're not."

"Damn it." He fell back against the pillows and stared up at the sheers gathered together at the ceiling. "I thought for sure I was having a breakthrough."

Kate swallowed. He was remembering, but the memory was just a bit skewed. With the pregnancy lie from his ex still fresh, Kate figured it was only a matter of time before he had full recollection of the situation.

She didn't know whether to be terrified or relieved. They still hadn't slept together, so she prayed their relationship could be redeemed once the old Luc returned.

"It just seemed so real," he went on. "My hand was on your stomach, and I was so excited to be a father. I had no clue what to do, but the idea thrilled me."

Her heart swelled to near bursting at his reaction. The thought of having a baby with him made her giddy all over. But they were treading in dangerous territory. This was going to go downhill fast if she didn't do something. She might not be able to feed him his memories, but that didn't mean she couldn't find other ways to trigger him.

"How about we take the Jet Skis out for a bit?" she suggested.

His eyes drifted from the ceiling to her. "I don't want to go out right now."

Wow. She'd never known him to turn down anything on the water. Especially his Jet Ski or his boat. She needed to get him out of the house, away from the temptation of the bed, the shower…anyplace that might set the scene for seduction.

"Do you want to just go relax on the beach and do absolutely nothing?"

Though the thought of them lying next to each other wearing only swimsuits didn't seem like a great idea, now that she'd said it aloud. Granted, they'd seen each other that way before, but not with him thinking they were in love and planning holy matrimony…not to mention his promise to make love to her today.

A wide smile spread across his face. "I have an even better idea."

That naughty look was something she definitely recognized. He had a plan, and she didn't know if she should worry or just go along for the ride.

Six

Sweat poured off his head, his muscles burned and he was finally getting that rush he needed.

Kate grunted, sweat rolling off her, and he didn't recall ever seeing her look more beautiful. Of course, he didn't recall much, but right at this moment, she was positively stunning.

"I can't do this anymore," she panted, falling back against the wall.

Luc eased the sledgehammer down to rest, the wood handle falling against his leg. "We can take a break."

"I kind of meant I can't do this anymore…ever."

Luc laughed. They'd just torn out the old vanity in the main bathroom off the hallway, and the scene was a disaster. The construction workers had left the majority of their smaller tools here, so he figured he'd do something useful while he waited for his memory to return. No, he'd never done any home projects before.

He was a prince, for crying out loud. But he knew this bathroom would be gutted and replaced, so he was just blowing off some steam while helping the workers along at the same time.

"What are we going to do with all of this mess?" Kate asked as she glanced around the room.

They stood amid a pile of broken ceramic material, some huge hunks and some shards.

"Leave it," he told her. "When the guys come back to finish this, they can haul it out."

She dropped her hammer on top of the disaster and turned to stare at him. "So we're just causing destruction and closing the door on our way out?"

Luc shrugged. "I'm not really known for my renovating skills. Am I?"

Kate laughed, swiping a hand across her forehead. "No. You're royalty. I don't know of too many blue bloods who go around remodeling."

Stepping over the debris, he made his way to the door. Kate was right behind him. Extending his hand, he helped her over the rubble and out into the hallway.

"How about we take our tools to the kitchen?" he said, smiling when she rolled her eyes. "That room is hideous."

"I'd rather go to the kitchen and make some lunch, because you only had coffee for breakfast and my toast wore off about my fifth swing into that vanity countertop."

Her glistening forehead, the smudge of dirt streaked across one cheek, instantly had Luc recalling a little girl with a lopsided ponytail chasing a dog through a yard.

"You used to play with Booker," he muttered, speaking before he fully finished assessing the image. "At my family's vacation house in the US."

Kate's eyes widened. "That's right. I did. Did you have a memory?"

Rubbing his forehead, Luc cursed beneath his breath when the flash was gone. "Yeah. I've known you a long time, then."

Kate nodded, studying him. "I've known you since I was six."

"I'm a lot older than you."

A smile spread across her face. "Ten years."

"How long have we been together?"

Kate glanced away, biting her lip and focusing on anything but him.

"I know the doctor said to let me remember on my own. But I want to know."

Those doe eyes came back up to meet his gaze. "I started working for you a year ago."

Shock registered first. "You work for me?"

He tried to remember, tried to think of her in a professional atmosphere. Nothing. He'd actually rather remember her in an intimate setting, because that was what crushed him the most. They were engaged, they were obviously in love and he couldn't recall anything about the deep bond of their relationship.

"What do you do for me?" he asked. "Besides get me hot and make me want you. And how did we manage to get around the family rule about not mixing business with pleasure?"

Pink tinged her tanned face as she reached out, cupping her hand over his cheek. "I'm your assistant. I'm not telling you anything else. All right?"

Sliding his hand over hers, he squeezed it, then brought her palm to his mouth. "All right," he said, kissing her. "But I can't believe I let my fiancée work."

Her lips quirked. "Let me? Oh, honey. You've never let me do anything."

Laughing, he tugged her against him. "I have a feeling we do a lot of verbal sparring."

A lopsided grin greeted him. "You have no idea."

When he started to nuzzle the side of her neck, she eased back. "I'm sweaty and smelly, Luc. I don't think you want to bury your nose anywhere near my skin right now."

He slid his tongue along that delicate spot just below her ear. "I plan on having you sweaty later anyway, Kate."

Her body trembled. He didn't need to spell out how their day would end. Sleeping next to her last night had been sweet torture, but seeing her come apart at his touch had been so erotic, so sexy.

He couldn't wait to have her. Couldn't wait to explore her, get to know her body all over again.

"Has it always been this intense between us?" he asked, still gripping her hand and staring into those eyes any man could get lost in.

"Everything about our relationship is intense," she murmured, staring at his mouth. "I never know if I want to kiss you or strangle you."

"Kissing," he whispered against her mouth. "Always choose kissing, my *doce anjo.*"

Sweet angel. Had he always called her that? When her lips parted beneath his, he knew the term was accurate. She tasted so sweet each time he kissed her. Wrapping one arm around her waist, he slid his palm over her backside. She still wore that short little sundress she'd had on all morning. She hadn't changed when they'd done the bathroom demolition, and seeing her bent over, catching a glimpse of her creamy thighs, had nearly driven him crazy.

Gathering the material beneath his hand, he cupped her bottom. "I've wanted you since last night," he muttered against her mouth. "The need for you hasn't lessened, and I may not remember our intimacy before, but something tells me I've been infatuated with you for a long time. This ache inside me isn't new."

A shaky sigh escaped her. "That's something I can't attest to. I don't know how long you've wanted me."

Luc eased back, still holding on to her backside. "Forever, Kate. I refuse to believe anything else."

Moisture gathered in her eyes. "You might end up remembering differently."

Then she stepped away, leaving him cold and confused. What did that mean? Did they not have a solid relationship, a deep love, as he'd thought?

Luc let her go. Apparently, they both had emotional demons to work through. Regardless of his temporary amnesia, he wouldn't let her go through this alone. They both needed each other, that was obvious, and even if she tried to push him away, she'd soon find out he wasn't going anywhere.

They were in this together no matter how he'd been before. She was his and he would be strong for her. He would not let this memory loss rob him of his life or his woman.

Kate threw on her suit and headed down to the beach. Luc might have been content with busting things up as a stress reliever, but she needed a good workout. There was nothing like a swim to really get the muscles burning and endorphins kicking in.

She hadn't lied when she'd told him their relationship had always been intense. And she hadn't lied when she'd said she had no clue how long he'd been infatuated with her.

But he was right about one thing. The emotions he was feeling, his actions toward her, weren't new. All that desire, that passion, had been lying dormant for some time now, and she'd wondered if it would ever break the surface. Never in her wildest dreams had she imagined it would take a major injury to further exacerbate this chemistry.

The question now was were these feelings truly directed toward her, or were they left over from his ex? A year ago he'd admitted to an attraction, but had put the brakes on it because of their professional relationship and her parents working so closely with his family. And it was then that he'd explained in great detail why members of his family never dated or got involved with an employee. The list of reasons was lengthy: reputations on the line, the employee could turn and go to the media with a fabricated story... There was too much at stake—even Luc's crown in this case—to let staff in on their personal lives. Kate didn't have a clue how Luc and his ex had been in private. She actually tried to never think of that. But now she couldn't stop herself.

Did Luc really have such strong emotions for her? If so, how had he kept it bottled up all this time?

Kate loosened the knot on her wrap, letting the sheer material fall onto the sand. Running straight into the ocean, the world at her back, she wished she could run from this whole ordeal and stop lying to Luc. She wished she could kiss him and sleep in his bed and have him know it was her and not the fake fiancée he'd conjured up.

He'd said they would be sleeping together later. Dodging that was going to be nearly impossible.

She was in desperate need of advice. She'd wanted to phone her mother earlier, but the call hadn't been able to go through. She would try again later. More than anything Kate needed her mother's guidance. Holding back from Luc was pure torture. How could she say no to the one thing she'd fantasized about for so long?

The warm water slid over her body as she sliced her arms through the gentle waves. The hot sun beat down on her back and her muscles were already screaming from the quick workout.

Kate pushed herself further, breaking the surface to take another deep breath and catch her bearings. Panting heavily, she dived back in for more. She'd not fully worked through her angst just yet.

Before she knew it, she'd gone so far up the coastline she couldn't see Luc's home anymore. She swam to the shore, trudged through the sand and sank down onto dry land. Pulling her legs up against her chest, Kate wrapped her arms around her knees and caught her breath, willing the answers to come.

One thing was clear. She and Luc needed to stay away from the house as much as possible. With just the two of them alone, there was no chaperone, nobody else to offer a buffer. At least back at the palace there was a full staff of butlers, maids, drivers, assistants to the assistants, guards, his parents, her parents, the cooks... the list was almost endless.

Perhaps an outing to the small village was in order. Anything to hold off the inevitable. The hungry look in Luc's eyes, the way he constantly kept touching her, were all indications that the moment was fast approaching. And yes, she wanted that moment to happen more than she wanted her next breath, but she didn't want it to be built on desperation and lies.

Pushing herself up off the sand, Kate stretched out her muscles. She'd never been a fan of running, but she wasn't done exorcising those demons. She headed back toward Luc's home, passing other pristine beach houses. Some were larger, some smaller, but they all had the same Mediterranean charm, and their own docks, with boats bobbing against the wood planks.

The island was a perfect getaway for a prince. Under normal circumstances, he could hide away here without the media hounding him, without the distractions of the internet and the outside world.

This place would be heaven on earth for any couple wanting a romantic escape.

Too bad she was only a figment of Luc's imagination.

As Kate ran, she kept to the packed sand that the waves had flattened. Her thigh muscles burned and sweat poured off her as the sun beat against her back. This felt good, liberating. She would go back to the house and go over Luc's schedule for when they returned to Ilha Beleza. Looking at all his duties and responsibilities would surely help jog something in his mind.

And the memories were returning. Apparently, her dirty state earlier had shot him back to the moments when she'd been a little girl and had gone to work with her parents. She'd loved the Silvas' old sheepdog, Booker. She used to play with him, roll around in the yard with him and be completely filthy by the time she left.

Luc's parents would just laugh, saying how they missed having a little one around. They'd gotten Booker when Luc was eight, so by the time he was a teen, he wasn't so much into running through yards and spending hours playing with a dog.

Kate was all about it. When Booker had passed away, she had taken the news harder than Luc had. Of course, he'd had his women "friends" to occupy his time and keep his thoughts focused elsewhere.

Finding her discarded wrap in the sand where she'd dropped it, Kate scooped it up and quickly adjusted it around her torso. At the base of the steps leading up to Luc's home, she rested her hands on her knees and pulled in a deep gulp of air. She was going in as professional Kate. Keeping her hands and mind off Luc was the only way to proceed. Flirty, dreamy Kate had no place here. They hadn't made love yet, so she could still turn this around, and pray Luc wasn't totally furious once he remembered what her role in his life actually was.

Seven

Luc's phone bounced on the couch cushion when he tossed it aside. Useless. He recognized his parents' names, his best friend, Mikos, and Kate. Other than that, nothing.

Raking a hand down his face, Luc got to his feet and crossed to the patio doors. Kate had been gone awhile and he knew her frustrations had driven her out the door. He'd like to run from his problems, too; unfortunately, they lived inside his head. Still, he couldn't fault her for needing some time alone.

He stepped out onto the patio, his gaze immediately darting down to the dock. As he stared at the Jet Ski on one side and his boat on the other, he wondered what he'd been doing before he fell. Was he about to go out on the water so late in the evening? Was Kate coming with him? Everything before the fall was a complete blank to him. He had no idea what they'd been doing prior to his accident.

Hell, he couldn't even recall how he and Kate had started working together. And some family rule about not getting personal with staff members kept ringing in his head. He reached into his mind, knowing this was a real memory. The Silva family didn't get intimate with employees. So had Kate come to work for him after they'd become a couple? Had she been so invaluable in his life that he'd wanted her to be his right-hand woman in his professional world, as well?

The questions weren't slowing down; they were slamming into his head faster than he could comprehend them. He'd go mad if he didn't get his memory back soon, or if he kept dwelling on something that was out of his control.

Damn it. Of one thing he was certain. Losing control of anything was pure hell, and right now he'd spiraled so far he hoped and prayed he could pull back the reins on his life before this amnesia drove a wedge between him and Kate.

Luc straightened as the idea slammed into him, pushing through the uncertainty he'd been battling. All that mattered was him and Kate. This was their time away, so all he had to do was enjoy being with her. How hard could that be? A private getaway with one sexy fiancée would surely be just what he needed.

A shrill ring came from the living room. Luc ran in and found Kate's cell phone on one of the end tables. His mother's name was on the screen. Odd that she would be calling Kate.

Without giving it another thought, he answered. "Hello."

"Lucas? Darling, how are you feeling?"

His mother's worried tone came over the line. Her

familiar voice had him relieved that his mind hadn't robbed him of that connection.

"Frustrated," he admitted, sinking onto the worn accent chair. "I have a hell of a headache, but other than that I feel fine. Why did you call Kate's phone?"

"I didn't want to bother you if you weren't feeling good, or if you were resting. I spoke with Kate last night, but I needed to check on you today."

"There's no need to worry, Mom. Kate is taking good care of me and the doctor was thorough. I just need to relax, and this is the best place for me to do that."

His mother made a noise, something akin to disapproval. "Well, you call the doctor first thing if you start having other symptoms. I'm still not happy you're not home. I worry, but you're stubborn like your father, so I'm used to it."

Luc smiled, just as Kate stepped through the door. A sheen of sweat covered her. Or maybe that was water from the ocean. Regardless, she looked sexy, all wet and winded. Would his need for her ever lessen? Each time he saw her he instantly went into primal mode and wanted to carry her back to bed.

"Nothing to worry about," he said, keeping his eyes locked on Kate's. "I'm in good hands. I'll phone you later."

He ended the call and rose to his feet. Kate's eyes widened as he moved closer to where she'd stopped in the doorway.

"Were you on my phone?" she asked, tipping her head back to hold his gaze.

"My mom called to check on me. She tried your cell in case I was resting."

Kate's eyes darted around. "Um…is that all she said?"

Reaching out to stroke a fingertip along her collarbone, Luc watched the moisture disappear beneath his touch. "Yes. Why?"

"Just curious." She trembled beneath his touch as her eyes locked back onto his. "I need to go shower. Then we need to discuss your schedule and upcoming events."

Heat surged through him as he slid his mouth over hers. "Go use my shower. We can work later."

She leaned into him just slightly, then quickly pulled back. Something passed through her eyes before she glanced away. As she started to move around him, he grabbed her elbow.

"You okay?"

She offered a tight, fake smile. "Fine. Just tired from my swim and run."

The shadows beneath her eyes silently told him she hadn't slept as well as she'd claimed. He nodded, releasing her arm, and listened as she padded through the hall and into the master suite.

Waiting until he was sure she was in the shower, Luc jerked his shirt over his head and tossed it, not caring where it landed. By the time he reached his bedroom, his clothes were gone, left in a trail leading to the bedroom door.

The steady hum of the water had Luc imagining all kinds of possibilities. And all of them involved a wet, naked Kate.

When he reached the spacious, open shower, surrounded by lush plants for added privacy, he took in the entire scene. Kate with water sluicing down her curves, her wet hair clinging to her back as she tipped her face up to the rainfall showerhead. She was a vision...and she was his.

Luc crossed the room and stepped onto the wet, gritty

tile. In an instant he had his arms wrapped around her, molding her back against him.

Kate's audible gasp filled the room, and her body tensed beneath his. "Luc—"

He spun her around, cutting off anything she was about to say. He needed her, needed to get back to something normal in his life. Kate was his rock, his foundation, and he wanted to connect with her again in the most primal, natural way possible.

"Luc," she muttered against his mouth. "We shouldn't."

Her words died as he kissed his way down her neck. "We should."

That silky skin of hers was driving him insane. Kate arched into him, gripping his shoulders as if holding on.

"You're injured," she panted.

He jerked his head up to meet her gaze. "The day I can't make love to my fiancée is the day I die."

Luc hauled her up against him, an arm banded around her lower back to pull her in nice and snug, as his mouth claimed hers once again. There was a hesitancy to her response. Luc slowed his actions, not wanting her to feel she needed to protect him.

But this all-consuming need to claim her, to have her right now, had his control slipping.

"I want you, Kate," he whispered against her mouth. "Now."

Nipping at her lips, he slid his palms over her round hips, to the dip in her waist and up to her chest, which was made for a man's hands...his hands. She was perfect for him in every way. How had he gotten so lucky to have her in his life?

As he massaged her, she dropped her head back, exposing that creamy skin on her neck. Luc smoothed his tongue over her, pulling a soft moan from her lips.

After backing her up, he lifted her. "Wrap your legs around me."

Her eyes went wide. "I… Luc…"

"Now, Kate."

Just as her legs encircled his waist, he grabbed her hands and held them above her head. Sliding into her, he stilled when she gasped.

"You okay?"

Eyes closed, biting down on her lip, she nodded. Luc gripped her wrists in one hand and used his other to skim his thumb across the lip she'd been worrying with her teeth.

"Look at me," he demanded. "I want to see those eyes."

Droplets sprinkled her lashes as she blinked up at him. He moved against her, watching her reaction, wanting to see every bit of her arousal, her excitement. He might not remember their past encounters, but he damn well was going to make new memories with her, starting right now.

Kate's hips rocked with his; her body arched as he increased his speed.

"Luc," she panted. "Please…"

Gripping her waist, he trailed his mouth up her neck to her ear. "Anything," he whispered. "I'll give you anything. Just let go."

Her body tensed, shuddering all around him. As she cried out in release, Luc followed her.

Wrapping her in his arms, he couldn't help but wonder if each time they were together felt like the first time, or if this particular moment was just so powerfully intense and all-consuming. This woman had the ability to bring him to his knees in all the right ways.

So why was his beautiful fiancée—who'd just come apart in his arms—sobbing against his shoulder?

* * *

Oh, no. No, no, no.

Kate couldn't stop the tears from coming, just as she couldn't stop Luc from making love to her.

No. Not making love. They'd had sex. He didn't love her, and once his memory returned, he wouldn't even like her anymore. She'd been worried about tonight, about going to sleep. She'd truly never thought he would join her in the shower. The sex just now with Luc was unlike any encounter she'd ever had. Nothing could have prepared her for the intensity of his passion.

How had this entire situation gotten even more out of control? The reality of being with Luc had far exceeded the fantasy. And now that she had a taste of what it could be like, she wanted more.

"Kate?"

She gripped his biceps, keeping her face turned into his chest. She couldn't face him, couldn't look him in the eyes. Not after what she'd done. He would never understand.

Was this how he'd treat her if he loved her? Would he surprise her in the shower and demand so much of her body? Part of her wanted to bask in the glorious aftermath of everything intimacy should be. But she knew it couldn't last.

Luc shut off the water behind her, and in one swift move, he shifted, lifting her in his arms.

"Talk to me, baby." He stepped out of the shower and eased her down onto the cushioned bench. Grabbing a towel from the heated bar, he wrapped it around her before securing one around his waist.

Kate stared down at her unpainted nails. Focusing on her lack of manicure would not help her out of this situation. Luc gripped her hands as he crouched before her.

"Look at me."

Those words, said only moments ago under extremely different circumstances, pulled her gaze away from their joined hands and up into his dark eyes. Worry stared back at her. Didn't he know she was lying? Didn't he know he should be worried about himself?

She could come clean. She could tell him right now that she wasn't his fiancée, that she'd been dying for him to make a move on her for years. But all that sounded even more pathetic than the truth, which was that she'd gotten caught up in this spiral of lies. In an attempt to protect him, she'd deceived him. There was no turning back, and if she was honest with herself, she couldn't deny how right they'd felt together.

"Did I hurt you?" he asked.

Swiping the moisture from her cheeks, Kate shook her head. "No. You could never hurt me."

"What is it? Did you not want to make love with me?"

A vise around her heart squeezed.

She shook her head. Eventually she was going to strangle herself with this string of lies.

"I'm just overwhelmed," she admitted. "We hadn't been together before."

Luc studied her a moment before his brows rose. "You mean to tell me we hadn't made love before?"

Shame filled her. She couldn't speak, so simply nodded.

Luc muttered a slang Portuguese term that no member of the royal family should be heard saying.

"How is that possible?" he asked. "You said we've been working together for nearly a year."

"Your family has a rule about staff and royal members not being intimate. We've been professional for so long, we both just waited. Then we ended up here on this getaway and..."

She couldn't finish. She couldn't lie anymore. The emotions were too overwhelming and her body was still reeling from their passion.

Luc came to his feet, cursing enough to have her cringing. He was beating himself up over something that was 100 percent her fault.

Unable to stand the tension, the heavy weight of the guilt, she jumped to her feet. "Luc, I need to tell you—"

"No." He turned, facing her with his hands on his narrow hips. "I took advantage of you. Kate, I am so, so sorry. I had no clue. I got caught up in the moment and wanted to forget this memory loss and just be with you."

"No. This is not your fault in any way." Holding on to the knot on her towel, Kate shivered. "Let's get dressed. We need to talk."

Eight

Luc grabbed his clothes from the bedroom and went to the spare room to get dressed. Of all the plans he'd had for Kate, taking her when she wasn't mentally prepared for it sure as hell wasn't one of them.

Their history explained why she'd tensed when he'd come up behind her in the shower, explained the onslaught of tears afterward. Not to mention the way she'd stiffened against him in bed last night.

Luc cursed himself once again for losing control. He'd thought he was doing the right thing, thought he was getting them both back to where they'd been just before his ridiculous accident.

Heading back down the hallway, he spotted his clothes. Looking at them now he felt only disgust, as opposed to the excitement and anticipation he'd felt when he'd left them behind without a care.

He grabbed each article of clothing and flung them

and his towel into the laundry area. He'd worry about that mess later. Right now he had another, more important mess to clean up, and he only hoped Kate would forgive him.

Guilt literally ate at him, killing the hope he'd had of making this day less about his amnesia and more about them.

By the time she came out, she'd piled her hair atop her head and sported another one of those little sundresses that showcased her tanned shoulders and sexy legs. The legs he'd demanded she wrap around him.

Kate took a seat on the sofa and patted the cushion beside her. "Just relax. Okay?"

Relax? How could he when this entire mess had started with him forgetting every single damn thing about the woman he supposedly loved?

Wait, he *did* love her. When he looked at her and saw how amazing and patient she was with him, and damn it, how she'd let him take her in the shower, and didn't stop him, how could he not love her? When he looked at her, his heart beat a bit faster. When he touched her, his world seemed to be a better place.

He just wished he could remember actually falling in love with her, because all he could recall was this all-consuming, aching need that was only stronger now that he'd had her.

"Luc." Kate held out her hand. "Come on."

He crossed to her, took her hand and sank onto the couch beside her.

"Tell me you're okay," he started, holding her gaze. "Tell me I didn't hurt you physically or emotionally."

A soft smile spread across her face. "I already told you, I'm fine. You were perfect, Luc."

She held on to him, her eyes darting down to where their hands joined.

"Before you fell, we were fighting," she told him. "I take full responsibility for everything that's happened to you, so don't beat yourself up over the shower."

Luc squeezed her hand. "The shower was all on me. If we were fighting before my fall, then that took two, so don't place all of that blame on yourself."

Kate smiled. Her eyes lifted to his. "We could play this game all day," she told him, her smile dimming a bit. "But I need to talk to you."

"What's wrong?"

Her tone, the worry in her eyes, told him something major was keeping her on edge.

"There are so many things that you need to know, but I've been holding back because I don't want to affect your healing process."

Luc edged closer, wrapping an arm around her shoulders and pulling her to his side. Easing back against the cushions, he kept her tucked against him. "If something is worrying you, tell me. I want to be here for you. I want to be strong for you."

Kate's delicate hand rested on his thigh. She took a deep breath in, then let it out with a shudder.

"I was adopted."

Her voice was so soft, he wondered if she actually meant to say it out loud.

"Did I already know this about you?" he asked.

"No. The only people who know are my parents."

His mind started turning. Her parents worked for his parents. Memories of them in his house flashed for an instant.

"Scott and Maria, right?"

"Yes." Kate tilted her head up to meet his gaze. "You're remembering."

"Not fast enough," he muttered. "Go on."

Settling her head back against his chest, Luc wondered if it was easier for her to talk if she wasn't looking right at him.

"I was born in the States," she went on. "Georgia, to be exact. My parents adopted me when I was six. I only have vague memories of being there, but it's always held a special place in my heart."

Luc listened, wondering where she was going with this and how it all tied back into what was happening between them now.

"My parents ended up moving to Ilha Beleza to work full-time at the palace. They used to just work at the vacation home back in Georgia. Your family has one off the coast."

Closing his eyes, he saw a white house with thick pillars extended to the second story. A wraparound porch on the ground floor had hanging swings that swayed in the breeze. Booker and a young Kate running in the yard...

Yes, he remembered that house fondly.

"Since I've been your assistant, I've wanted you to visit that orphanage, the one I came from, but we've butted heads over it."

Luc jerked, forcing Kate to shift and look up at him.

"Why were we fighting over an orphanage?" he asked.

She shrugged. "I have no idea why you won't go. To be honest, I just think you don't want to, or you didn't want to take the time. You've offered to write a check, but I never can get you to go there. I just felt a visit from a real member of royalty would be something cool for those kids. They don't have much and some of them have been there awhile, because most people only want to adopt babies."

Luc glanced around the sparsely furnished room, hoping for another flash of something to enter his mind. Hoping for some minuscule image that would help him piece it all together.

"Is this why we were arguing before I fell?" he asked, focusing back on her.

"Not really. I tried bringing it up again, but you blew it off." She let go of his hand and got to her feet, pacing to the open patio doors. "We were arguing because we're both stubborn, and sometimes we do and say things before we can fully think them through."

He could see that. Without a doubt he knew he was quite a hardhead, and Kate had a stubborn streak he couldn't help but find intriguing and attractive.

"When your memory comes back, I want you to know that everything I've ever done or said has been to protect you." Her shoulders straightened as she kept her back to him and stared out the doors. "I care about you, Luc. I need you to know that above all else."

The heartfelt words, the plea in her tone, had Luc rising to his feet and crossing to her. Placing his hands on her shoulders, he kissed the top of her head.

"I know how you feel about me, Kate. You proved it to me when you let me make love to you, when you put my needs ahead of any doubts you had."

She eased back against him. "I hope you always feel that way."

The intensity of the moment had him worried they were getting swept into something so consuming, they'd never get back to the couple they used to be. Even though he didn't remember that couple, he had to assume they weren't always this intense.

"What do you say we take the boat and go into town?" he asked. "Surely there's a market or shops or restaurants to occupy our time. We need to have some fun."

She turned in his arms, a genuine smile spreading across her face. "I was going to suggest that myself. I haven't shopped in forever. I'm always working."

She cringed, as if she just realized what had come out of her mouth.

"It's okay," he told her, kissing the tip of her nose. "I'll make sure your boss gives you the rest of the day off. You deserve it."

That talk didn't go nearly the way she'd rehearsed it in her head. Coming off the euphoria of having mind-blowing sex with Luc in the shower had seriously clouded her judgment, and obviously sucked out all her common sense.

So now here she was, wearing her favorite blue halter dress, letting the wind blow her hair around her shoulders and face while Luc steered his boat to the main dock of the island's small town. Most people traveled by boat to the village, where scooters were the preferred mode of transportation. The marina was lined with crafts of various sizes and colors. As they'd made their way toward the waterfront, they'd passed by other boaters and waved. Kate really liked this area. Too bad she'd probably never be back after the mess she'd created came crashing down on her.

Through her research she knew the locals would line up along the narrow streets, set up makeshift booths and sell their goods. From what she'd seen online, she might find anything from handmade jewelry and pottery to flowers and vegetables. She was excited to see what caught her fancy, perhaps taking her mind off the fact her body was still tingling from Luc's touch.

She'd never be able to shower again—especially in that master bath—without feeling his body against hers, his breath on her shoulders. Without hearing his demanding words in her ear as he fully claimed her.

Then he'd let his guard down and opened up to her about his feelings. Slowly, she was falling in love with the man she'd been lying to, the man who was off-limits in reality. She'd opened up about her past, wanting to be as honest as she could in an area that had nothing to do with what was happening right now.

Luc secured the boat to the dock, then extended his hand to help her out. With a glance or simple touch, the man had the ability to make her stomach quiver, her heart quicken and her mind wander off into a fantasy world. Still, that was no excuse to have let the charade go this far.

There was no going back now, though. The charade may be all a farce, but her emotions were all too real.

Kate knew she should've told Luc about the false engagement when he'd hinted that he wanted to make love to her. She should've told him right that moment, but she hadn't, and now here she was on the other side of a monumental milestone they would both have to live with.

She was falling for him; there was no denying the truth to herself. What had started as physical attraction long ago had morphed into more because of his untimely incident.

How did she keep her heart protected, make sure Luc stayed safe until he remembered the truth on his own and keep hold of the man she'd come to feel a deeper bond for? There was no good way this scenario would play out. Someone was going to get hurt.

"You okay?" Luc asked, hauling her onto the dock beside him.

Pasting on a smile, Kate squeezed his hand. "Fine. Let's see what this island has to offer."

Other boats bobbed up and down in the water on either side of the long dock. Luc led her up the steps to the street. Once they reached the top, Kate gasped. It was like a mini festival, but from all she'd heard about this quaint place, the streets were always this lively.

Brightly colored umbrellas shaded each vendor. A small band played live music in an alcove of one of the ancient buildings. People were laughing, dancing, and nearly every stand had a child behind the table, working alongside an adult. Obviously, this was a family affair.

Kate tamped down that inner voice that mocked her. Her dream was to raise a family, to have a husband who loved her, to watch their babies grow. Maybe someday she'd have that opportunity. Unfortunately, with the way her life was going now, she'd be looking for a new job as opposed to a spouse.

Suddenly, one of the stands caught her eye. "Oh, Luc." She tugged on his hand. "I have to get a closer look."

She practically dragged him down the brick street to the jewelry booth. The bright colors were striking with the sun beating down on them just so. It was as if the rays were sliding beneath the umbrella shading the area. The purple amethyst, the green jade, the yellow citrine—they were all so gorgeous. Kate didn't know which piece she wanted to touch first.

"Good afternoon."

The vendor greeted her in Portuguese. Kate easily

slid into the language as she asked about the wares. Apparently, the woman was a widow and the little girl sidling up against her was her only child. They made the jewelry together and the girl was homeschooled, oftentimes doing lessons right there at the booth.

Kate opened her small clutch to pull out her money. There was no way she could walk away and not buy something from this family.

Before she could count her cash, Luc placed a hand over hers and shook his head. He asked the lady how much Kate owed for the necklace and earrings she'd chosen. Once he paid and the items were carefully wrapped in red tissue paper, they went on their way to another booth.

"You didn't have to pay," she told him. "I don't expect you to get all of the things I want, Luc."

He shrugged, taking her hand and looping it through his elbow as they strolled down the street. "I want to buy you things, Kate."

"Well, I picked these out for my mother," she said with a laugh.

Luc smiled. "I don't mind buying things for my future mother-in-law, either. Really, think nothing of it."

What had been a beautiful, relaxing moment instantly turned and smacked Kate in the face with a dose of reality. A heavy ball of dread settled in her belly. This was getting all too real. Kate's parents had been inadvertently pulled into this lie. They would never be Luc's in-laws, and once he discovered the truth, they might not even be employees of his family.

They moved to another stand, where the pottery was unique, yet simple. Kate eyed a tall, slender vase, running her hand over the smooth edge. Before she knew it, Luc had paid for it and the vendor was bagging it and wrapping it in several layers of tissue for protection.

"You don't have to buy everything I look at," she informed Luc.

"Did you like the piece?" he asked.

"I love it, but I was wondering what it would look like in your new house."

Luc kissed her softly on the lips before picking up the bag and moving away. "Our house, Kate. If you like it, then it's fine with me. I'm not much of a decorator."

"No, you prefer to demolish things."

Luc laughed. "Actually, our little project was my first experiment in destruction, but I did rather enjoy myself. I really think I'll tackle that kitchen before we leave, and give the contractors a head start."

They moved from place to place, eyeing various trinkets. Kate ended up buying a wind chime and fresh flowers while Luc was busy talking to another merchant. She wanted to liven up the dining area in the house, especially since the room was in desperate need of paint. The lavender flowers would look perfect in that new yellow vase.

Once they had all their bags, they loaded up the boat and headed home.

Home. As if this was a normal evening and they were settled in some married-couple routine. Kate shouldn't think of Luc's house as her home. She'd started getting too settled in, too comfortable with this whole lifestyle, and in the end, when her lie was exposed and his inevitable rejection sliced her in two, she would have nobody to blame but herself.

These past few hours with Luc had been amazing, but her fantasy life wouldn't last forever.

Nine

Sometime during the past hour, Kate had fully detached herself. She'd been quiet on the boat, quiet when they came into the house. She'd arranged fresh flowers in that beautiful yellow vase and placed them on the hideous dining room table without saying a word.

She'd made dinner, and the only sound he'd heard was her soft humming as she stirred the rice. Now they'd finished eating, and Luc couldn't handle the silence anymore.

He had something to say.

"Kate."

She stepped from the kitchen, wiping her hands down her dress. Luc remained standing, waited for her to cross to him.

"I know you've got a lot on your mind right now," he started. "But there's something I need to tell you."

"Wait." She held up a palm. "I need to go first. I've

been trying to figure out a way to talk to you about your amnesia."

She sighed, shaking her head. "I don't even know how to start," she muttered. "I've racked my brain, but nothing sounds right."

"The doctor said not to prompt me." Luc reached into his pocket and pulled out a small, velvet pouch. "While you're thinking about the right words, why don't you take this?"

She jerked her gaze up to his, then stared down at the present in his hand. "What is it?"

"Open it."

Her fingers shook as she took the pouch and tugged on the gathered opening. With a soft gasp, she reached in and pulled out an emerald-cut amethyst ring.

"Luc." She held the ring up, stared at it, then looked to him. "What's this for?"

"Because you don't have a ring on your finger. It hit me today, and I don't know why you don't, but I didn't want to wait and find out. I saw this and I knew you'd love it."

When she didn't say anything or put the ring on, his nerves spiked. Strange, since he'd obviously already popped the question. Unless she just didn't like it.

"If you'd rather have something else, I can take it back to the lady and exchange it. When I saw that stone, I remembered something else about you."

Her eyes widened. "You did?"

A tear slipped down her cheek as she blinked. Luc swiped it away, resting his hand on the side of her face. "I remembered your birthday is in February and that's your birthstone. I remembered you have this amethyst pendant you've worn with gowns to parties at the palace. That pendant would nestle right above your breasts. I used to be jealous of that stone."

Kate sucked in a breath as another tear fell down her face. "You say things like that to me and I feel like you've had feelings for me for longer than I ever imagined."

Taking the ring from her hand, he slid it onto her left ring finger. "There are many things I don't remember, but I know this—I've wanted you forever, Kate."

He didn't give her a chance to respond. Luc enveloped her in his arms, pulled her against him and claimed her mouth. He loved kissing her, loved feeling her lush body against his. Nothing had ever felt this perfect, as far as he could recall. And he was pretty sure if anything had ever felt this good, he'd remember.

Kate's hands pushed against his shoulders as she broke the kiss. "Wait."

She turned, coming free from his hold. With her rigid back to him, Luc's nerves ramped up a level. "Kate, what's wrong?"

"I want to tell you," she whispered. "I need to tell you, but I don't know how much I can safely say without affecting your memory."

Taking a step toward her, he cupped his hands over her shoulders. "Then don't say anything. Can't we just enjoy this moment?"

She turned in his arms, stared up at him and smiled. "I've never been happier than I am right now. I just worry what will happen once you remember everything."

His lips slid across hers. "I'm not thinking of my memory. I only want to make up for what we did this morning."

A catch in her breath had him pausing. Her eyes locked onto his.

"I want to make love to you properly, Kate."

Her body shuddered beneath his hands. "I've wanted you for so long, Luc."

Something primal ripped through him at the same time he saw a flash of Kate wearing a fitted skirt suit, bending over her desk to reach papers. He shook off the image. She'd already said she was his assistant, so that flash wasn't adding anything new to the mix.

Right now he had more pressing matters involving his beautiful fiancée.

"I want you wearing my ring, the weight of my body and nothing else."

Luc gave the halter tie on her neck a tug, stepping back just enough to have the material floating down over her bare breasts. With a quick yank, he pulled the dress and sent it swishing to the floor around her feet. Next he rid her of her silky pink panties.

With her hair tossed around her shoulders, her mouth swollen from his kisses, Luc simply stared at her, as if taking all this in for the first time.

"Perfect," he muttered, gliding his hands over her hips and around her waist. "Absolutely perfect and totally mine."

The breeze from the open patio doors enveloped them. The sunset just on the horizon created an ambience even he couldn't have bought. And everything about this moment overshadowed all that was wrong in his mind with the amnesia.

Guiding Kate backward, he led her to a chaise. When her legs bumped against the edge, Luc pressed on her shoulders, silently easing her down. Once she lay all spread out for his appreciation, he started tugging off his own clothes. The way her eyes traveled over his body, studying him, did something to his ego he couldn't explain. He found himself wanting to know what she thought when she looked at him, what she felt. All this was still new to him and he wanted to savor every single moment of their lovemaking.

"I've dreamed of this," he murmured.

Her brows quirked. "Seriously? You don't think it was a memory of something?"

Luc rested one hand on the back of the chaise, another on the cushion at her hip. As he loomed over her, his body barely brushed the tips of her breasts.

"I'm sure," he whispered. "You were on my balcony, naked, smiling. Ready for me."

A cloud of passion filled her eyes as she continued to stare up at him.

"Maybe I had that fantasy when I first looked at this place, or maybe I had that vision since we've been here." He nipped at her collarbone, gliding up her exposed throat. "Either way, you were meant to be here. With me. Only me."

Kate's body arched into his as her fingertips trailed up his biceps and rested at his shoulders. "Only you," she muttered.

Luc eased down, settling between her legs. The moment his lips touched hers, he joined them, slowly taking everything she was willing to give. This all-consuming need he had for her only grew with each passing moment. Kate was in his blood, in his heart. Was it any wonder he wanted to marry her and spend his life with her?

Kate's fingertips dug into his skin as she rested her forehead against his shoulder. Luc knew from the little pants, the soft moans, that she was on the brink of release.

He kissed her neck, working his way up to that spot

behind her ear he already knew was a trigger. Her body clenched around him as she cried out his name. Before she stopped trembling, he was falling over the edge, too, wrapped in the arms of the woman he loved, surrounded by a haze of euphoria that kept away all the ugly worries and doubts.

All that mattered was Kate and their beautiful life together.

His hand slid over her flat stomach. There was a baby, his baby, growing inside her. He hadn't thought much about being a father, but the idea warmed something within him.

Dropping to his knees, he kissed her bare stomach. "I love you already," he whispered.

Luc jerked awake, staring into the darkness. What the hell was that? A memory? Just a random dream? His heart beat so fast, so hard against the wall of his chest. That had been real. The emotions, the feel of her abdomen beneath his palm, had all been real.

Luc wasn't one to believe in coincidences. That was a memory, but how could it be? Kate wasn't pregnant. She'd said they hadn't made love before the shower, so what the hell was that dream about?

Glancing at the woman beside him, Luc rubbed a hand over his face. The sheet was twisted around her bare body, and her hair was spread over the pillow. Luc placed a hand on her midsection and closed his eyes. That dream was so real he'd actually felt it.

Surely it wasn't just a fantasy of the day he and Kate would be expecting in real life.

He fell back against his pillow, laced his hands behind his head and blinked to adjust his eyesight to the darkened room. No way could he go back to sleep now.

There was too much on his mind, too many unanswered questions.

Something involving a baby had happened to cause such a strong flashback, for the second time now. It just didn't make sense. His mind was obviously the enemy at the moment.

"Luc..."

He turned toward her, only to find her eyes were still closed. She was dreaming, too. Her hand shifted over the sheets as if seeking him out. Instantly, he took hold of her hand and clasped it against his chest. Tomorrow he would have to seek some answers. This waiting around was killing him, because tidbits of his life weren't enough. He wanted the whole damn picture and he wanted it now.

Maybe if Kate talked about herself, her personal life, that would trigger more memories for him. He was done waiting, done putting his life in this mental prison.

How could he move on with Kate when he couldn't even remember their lives before a few days ago?

Ten

She should've told him. No matter what the doctor said, she should have just told Luc that they weren't engaged. Everything else he could remember on his own, but the biggest lie of all needed to be brought out into the open.

Of course, now they'd slept together twice, and she still hadn't said a word.

The heaviness of the ring on her hand wasn't helping the guilt weighing on her heart, either. Instead of trying to make this right, she'd let every single aspect spin even more out of control.

Stepping from the bathroom, Kate tied the short, silky robe around her waist. As soon as she glanced up, she spotted Luc sitting up in bed, the stark white sheet settled low around his hips. All those tanned, toned muscles, the dark ink scrolling over one shoulder, the dark hair splattering over his pecs. The man exuded sex appeal and authority.

"You needn't have bothered with that robe if you're going to keep looking at me like that," he told her, his voice husky from sleep.

Kate leaned against the door frame to the bathroom. "Did you know you never wanted to marry?" she asked, crossing her arms over her chest.

Luc laughed, leaning back against the quilted headboard. "That's a bit off topic, but no. I didn't know that."

Swallowing, Kate pushed forward. "You had no intention of taking a wife, but Ilha Beleza has some ridiculously archaic law that states you must be married by your thirty-fifth birthday in order to succeed to the throne."

"My birthday is coming up," he muttered, as if that tidbit just hit him. Luc's brows drew together as he laced his fingers over his abdomen. "Are you saying I'm not entitled to the throne if we aren't married by then?"

This was the tricky part. "You aren't crowned until you're married."

"That's ridiculous." He laughed. "I'll change that law, first thing. What if my son doesn't want to marry? Who says you have to be married by thirty-five?"

Kate smiled. "That's exactly what you said before you fell. You were dead set on having that law rewritten."

His eyes held hers another moment, but before she could go on, he said, "I had a dream last night. It was real. I know it was a memory, but I can't figure it out."

Kate's heart beat faster in her chest. Was their time over? Was the beautiful fantasy they'd been living about to come to a crashing halt?

"What was the dream?" she asked, gripping her arms with anticipation.

"I had a dream you were pregnant. That image in my

head has hit more than once." His eyes drilled into her. "Why would I keep dreaming that, Kate?"

"Did you see me in the dream?" she asked, knowing she was treading on very shaky ground.

He shook his head. "No. I had my hands on your bare stomach and I was so happy. Nervous, but excited."

"I've never been pregnant," she told him softly. "Do you think maybe you're just thinking ahead?"

Kate glanced away, unable to look him in the eyes and see him struggle with this entire situation. Why couldn't this be real? He'd told her more than once that he loved her, but that was just what he thought he was supposed to say...wasn't it? Still, what if he was speaking from his heart? What if that fall had actually pulled out his true feelings? But even if she stood a chance with the man she'd fallen in love with, Kate had lied and deceived him. He would never forgive her.

She just wanted today, just one more night with him. She was being selfish, yes, but she couldn't let go just yet. Not when everything right at this moment was beautiful and perfect.

"Do you want children?" he asked. "I assume we've discussed this."

Kate pushed herself off the door frame and smoothed her hair back from her face. "I do want kids. It's always been my dream to have a husband who loves me and a houseful of children."

He offered her a wide, sexy smile. "We will have the most beautiful children."

Oh, when he said things like that she wanted to get swept away and believe every word. Yet again, Luc had been weaved so tightly into this web of lies she'd inadvertently created. Her heart had been in the right place. She only hoped Luc saw that once all was said and done.

"I think any child with the Silva genes would be beautiful," she countered. "Even though you're an only child, your father has a long line of exotic beauties on his side. Your mother is a natural beauty, as well."

Luc tossed his sheet aside and came to his feet. Padding across the floor wearing only a tattoo and a grin, he kept his gaze on hers.

"As much as I'd love to work on those babies, I think I'd like to do something that will help get my memory back sooner rather than later."

Kate forced her gaze up... Well, she made it to his chest and figured that was a good compromise. "What's that?"

"Maybe we should tackle that work schedule you'd mentioned." His smile kicked up higher on one side of that kissable mouth. "You know, before we got sidetracked with being naked."

Kate laughed. "Yes. Work. That's where we need to focus."

Finally. Something they could do that actually needed to be done. She could breathe a bit now.

"I'll go get my laptop," she told him. "I've got a spreadsheet there of your tentative schedule, and I have a speech written out for you that you need to look over."

As she started to walk by, he reached out, snaking an arm around her waist. "You write my speeches?"

"For the past year I have."

His eyes roamed over her face, settled on her lips, then came back up to meet her gaze. "You really are perfect for me."

Kate swallowed. "Better put some clothes on. You can't work in your birthday suit."

His laughter followed her from the room, mocking her. She wasn't perfect for him. She wanted to be. Oh, mercy, how she wanted to be. She'd give him every-thing, but this dream romance was about to come to an end. His memories were coming back a little each day. Time was not on her side.

Maybe by focusing on work, he'd start to piece more things together. Perhaps then she wouldn't have to worry about saying anything. Honestly, she didn't know what scenario would be worse, her telling him the truth or him figuring it out on his own.

Was she a coward for not wanting to tell him? Absolutely. Not only did she not want to see that hurt—and quite possibly hatred—in his eyes, she didn't want that confrontation. There were no right words to say, no good way to come out and tell him he'd been living a complete lie for these past few days.

The end result would be the same, though, no matter how he found out. He would be disgusted with her. Suddenly, losing her job, or even her parents' positions, wasn't the main problem. After this time away from their ordinary lives, she couldn't imagine life without Luc.

And every bit of this scenario made her seem fool-ish, selfish and desperate.

When had she become that woman? When had she become the woman Luc had actually been engaged to? Because Kate was no better than his lying, scheming ex.

Luc glanced over Kate's shoulder as she sat in a patio chair with her laptop on the mosaic-tiled table. They'd opted to work outside to enjoy the bright sunshine and soft ocean breeze.

Resting his hands on the back of the chair, Luc leaned in to read over the tentative spreadsheet, but he was finding it impossible to focus. Kate's floral scent kept hitting him with each passing drift of wind.

"I can move these engagements around," Kate told him, pointing to the two green lines on the screen. "Both appointments are flexible. I scheduled them like this because I thought it would save time."

"Fine. You know more about this than I do," he told her.

She shifted, peeking at him over her shoulder. "I know about scheduling, but this is your life, Luc. Give me some input here. I can add or take away time. Usually, when you don't want to stay at an event too long, I make an excuse and cut the time back."

His brows quirked. "Seriously?"

"Well, yeah. How else would you escape and still look like the charming prince?" She laughed.

"Wow, you really do everything for me." With a sigh, he straightened. "What you have works for me. You've done this for a year, so you obviously know what you're talking about."

Kate turned fully in her chair and narrowed her eyes. "That's the Luc I used to work with. You never wanted to help with the schedule. You always trusted me to make it work."

Another flash of Kate in a snug suit, black this time, filled his mind. A dark-haired woman stood next to her. Luc closed his eyes, wanting to hold on to the image, needing to see who it was. Who was this woman?

Alana.

The image was gone as fast as it entered his mind, but he had a name.

"Luc?"

He opened his eyes, meeting Kate's worried gaze. She'd come to her feet and stood directly in front of him.

"Who's Alana?" he asked.

Kate jerked as if he'd slapped her. "Do you remember her?"

"I had a flash of you and her talking, but I couldn't tell what you guys were saying. It's like a damn movie that plays in my head with no sound."

He raked a hand down his face, meeting her eyes once more. "Who is she?" he repeated.

"She was a woman you used to date."

Luc tried to remember more, but nothing came to mind. Only that the woman's name stirred emotions of anger and hurt within him.

"Were we serious?" he asked.

Kate crossed her arms and nodded. "You were."

She was really sticking to the doctor's orders and not feeding him anything more than he was asking. Damn it, he wished she'd just tell him.

Pacing across the patio, Luc came to a stop at the edge by the infinity pool and stared out at the ocean. With the world at his back, he wished he could turn away from his problems so easily.

Alana Ferella. The name slid easily into his mind as he watched the waves roll onto the shore. His heart hardened, though. What kind of relationship had they had together? Obviously, not a compatible one or he'd still be with her. Something akin to rage settled in him. She hadn't been a nice woman, that much he knew.

He didn't want to keep asking Kate about an ex-girlfriend, and most likely Alana didn't matter, anyway. He just wished he could remember more about Kate, more about the plans they'd made.

"Are we getting married soon?" he asked, turning back to face her.

She blinked a few times, as if his question had thrown

her off. Hell, it probably had. He'd just gone from quizzing her on his ex to discussing their own nuptials.

"There's no set date," she told him.

That was weird. Once they'd announced their engagement, wouldn't the proper protocol have been to set a date? "Why not?" he asked. "With my birthday approaching, the throne in question and being a member of a royal family, I'm shocked we don't have something set."

Biting on her lip, Kate shrugged. "We can discuss the details in a bit. Can we finalize this schedule first? I'd like to make some calls later, if the cell service is working, to confirm your visit. I also need to let my dad know, so security can be arranged."

She was dodging his question for a reason. Did she simply not want to discuss things because of his memory loss, or was there something more to it? She'd admitted they'd argued before his fall. Had they been arguing over the wedding? Had they been arguing over…what? Damn it.

Smacking his palm on the table hard enough to make it rattle, Luc cursed, then balled his hands into fists. Kate jumped, taking a step back.

Kate started to step forward, but he held up a hand.

"No," he ordered. "Don't say anything. There's nothing you can do unless you want to tell me everything, which goes against the doctor's orders."

The hurt look on her face had him cursing. She was just as much a victim in this as he was.

"Kate, I didn't mean to lash out at you."

She shook her head, waving a hand. "It's okay."

"No, it's not." Closing the gap between them, he pulled her into his arms. "You've been here for me, you've done so much and I'm taking out my anger and frustrations on you when you're only trying to protect me."

Kate wrapped her arms around his waist. "I can handle it, Luc. It's partially my fault you're in this position, anyway. If we hadn't been arguing, if I hadn't made you so angry you went down to that wet dock, none of this would be happening."

Luc eased back. "None of this is your fault. At least pieces of my life are finally revealing themselves, and I'm sure it won't be long before the rest of the puzzle is filled in."

Kate had sacrificed so much for him. Yet he hadn't heard her tell him once that she loved him. Luc eased back, looking her in the eyes.

"Why are you marrying me?" he asked, stroking her jawline with his thumbs.

Her body tensed against his as her eyes widened. "What do you mean?"

"Do you love me?" he asked, tipping his head down a touch to hold her gaze.

Instantly, her eyes filled. Kate's hands came up, framed his face. "More than you'll ever know," she whispered.

Relief coursed through him. He didn't know why, but it was imperative to know her true feelings.

"I want to do something for you." She placed a light, simple kiss on his lips. "Tonight I'm going to make your favorite dinner. We're going to have a romantic evening and there will be no talk of the amnesia, the wedding, the work. Tonight will just be about Kate and Luc."

Wasn't that the whole point of this getaway? She cleverly circled them back around to the purpose of this trip. One of the many reasons he assumed he'd fallen in love with her. She kept him grounded, kept him on track.

Tugging her closer to him, he nuzzled her neck. "Then I expect one hell of a dessert," he growled into her ear.

Eleven

She had to tell him. There was no more stalling. The anguish, the rage that was brewing deep within Luc was more than she could bear. No matter what the doctor said, she had to come clean, because Luc getting so torn up had to be more damaging than just learning the truth.

And the truth beyond this whole messed-up situation was that she loved him. She hadn't lied when he'd asked. Kate had fallen completely in love with Luc and to keep this secret another day just wasn't acceptable.

She put on her favorite strapless green dress and her gold sandals. With her hair piled atop her head, she added a pair of gold-and-amethyst earrings.

A glance down at her hand had her heart clenching. He'd given her a ring. She wore a ring from a man she loved, yet he truly had no idea who she was.

At this point, she didn't recognize herself. She'd never been a liar or a manipulator. Yet here she was, doing a bang-up job of both.

Even with the patio doors open, the house smelled amazing with their dinner of fish and veggies baking in the oven. No matter how the evening ended, Kate wanted one last perfect moment with Luc.

Her mother would be relieved that Kate was finally telling the truth. What would Luc's parents say? Would they insist she be fired? Would they dismiss her parents from their duties as well, as she'd feared all along?

No matter the ramifications, Kate had to do the right thing here.

She headed to the kitchen to check the progress of dinner. When she glanced out toward the ocean, she noticed the darkening skies. Another storm rolling in. How apropos. Hadn't this entire nightmare started with a storm? For once in her life she wasn't looking forward to the added turmoil from Mother Nature.

Luc stood on the patio with his phone. Kate had no idea who he was talking to, but whoever it was, their call would be cut off soon due to this crazy weather.

Nerves settled deep in Kate's stomach. She wanted nothing more than to go back in time and have a redo of the night Luc fell. First of all, she never would've argued with him. If he didn't want to do the orphanage visit, fine. She'd been beating her head against that proverbial wall for nearly a year and he'd never given in. Why had she assumed he'd grow a heart all of a sudden and go?

Of course, now that he was drawing a blank on certain aspects of his life, he seemed to have forgotten how cold he used to be. Kate truly wished this Luc, the one she'd spent the past few days with, the one who had made love to her as if he truly loved her, was the Luc who would emerge after all the dust settled.

The worry eating at her would not help her be strong when she most needed to be. Everything that Luc threw at her would be justified, and right now she just needed to figure out the best way to come clean, because she truly didn't want to harm him any more than she had to.

After checking the dinner, she pulled the pan from the oven. Once she had their plates made, she started to call him, but realized he was still on the phone. The electricity flickered as rumbles of thunder resounded outside. Kate quickly searched for candles, because inevitably the lights were going to go. Perfect. It seemed Mother Nature was on her side. With the lights off, Kate wouldn't have to see the hatred on Luc's face when she told him that everything he knew about her, about them, was a lie.

"Darling, did you hear what I said?"

Luc concentrated on his mother's voice, the words she was saying, but something still didn't fit.

"You said Alana contacted you because she wants to see me," he repeated slowly, still trying to process all this.

Kate had told him Alana was an ex, but why would she be contacting him if he was engaged to Kate?

"Yes," his mother confirmed. "She's called me twice and she's very adamant that she wants to see you. I'm not going to stick my nose in this—you can respond however you want—but I don't think it's a good idea."

Luc's eyes locked onto the orange horizon. This view alone was reason enough to buy this property, no matter how many upgrades he wished to have inside. But right now, his head was pounding as if memories were rushing to the surface, waiting to get out all at once.

"Why would she contact you at all?" he asked. Resting one hand on the rail, he clutched the phone with his other, struggling to hear through the static. "Alana is in my past."

"So you remember her? Good. Then you don't need me to say how ridiculous this notion is that she can just come back into our lives after the entire baby scandal..."

His mother's voice cut out, but in the midst of her talking Luc did catch the word *baby.*

He rubbed his forehead. A flash of a diamond ring, a snippet of Alana in tears saying something about a pregnancy...

"To think she could trick you into marriage simply by saying she's pregnant was absurd," his mother went on, oblivious to his inner turmoil. "The timing of you purchasing this getaway house was perfect. Alana has no idea where you are."

The timing?

Luc spun around, glancing in through the open doors. Beyond the living area was the kitchen, where Kate stood preparing dinner. Instantly, he saw it all. His mother's single, damning word *timing* had triggered an avalanche of memories.

Kate was his assistant. No doubt about that, but they weren't engaged. They were strictly employee-employer, and that had been the extent of their relationship...until just a few days ago.

He felt sick to his stomach as he reached out, seeking the edge of a wrought-iron chair. He needed support, and right now all he could call upon was an inanimate object.

"Alana has no place in this family, Lucas."

Luc swallowed, his eyes remaining locked on Kate. Obviously, he'd been played by two women in his life—two women he'd trusted and let in intimately—on so many levels.

No wonder she was always so hesitant to let him in on his past. Kate's silence probably had little to do with the doctor's warnings and everything to do with her own agenda.

How could he have been so blind? How the hell could Kate have taken advantage of his vulnerability like that? Being manipulative wasn't like her, or at least not like the Kate he'd known. What had changed? Why had she felt it necessary to lie to his face, to go along with this charade that they were engaged?

Luc closed his eyes, gritting his teeth. "Mom, I'll call you back later. The connection is bad with the weather."

The call was cut off before he could finish. This storm was going to be a big one and he didn't just mean the one brewing outside.

Luc held the phone down at his side, dropped his head and tried like hell to forget the images, the emotions that went along with the fact he'd slept with Kate. He'd had sex with his assistant. He'd thought himself in love with her, believed that he'd be marrying her, making her the next queen.

She knew full well he didn't step over the line of professional boundaries. He'd outlined that fact for her a year ago when their attraction had crept to the surface, and he'd wanted to nip it in the bud. Kate knew every single thing about him and she'd used that to her advantage. She knew of the real fiancée, the fake pregnancy, and even after he'd brought up having visions of a baby, she'd said nothing.

How far would she have let this farce go? How long was she intending to lie straight to his face? Earlier she'd claimed she loved him.

Luc's heart clenched. Love had no place in the midst of lies and deceit.

Bringing his eyes back up, he caught her gaze across the open space. She smiled, a smile that he'd once trusted, and Luc felt absolutely nothing but disgust.

He knew exactly what he had to do.

When he hadn't returned her smile, Kate worried. Again she wondered who he'd been talking to on the phone. Something or someone had upset him.

Well, whatever it was, she couldn't let that hold her back. She couldn't keep finding excuses to put this discussion off.

"Dinner is ready," she called, setting the plates on the old, scarred table.

She glanced at the bouquet she'd purchased just the other day at the street market. She and Luc had shared so many amazing memories in such a short time, but she couldn't even relish them because they were built upon the lies she'd created using the feeble excuse that it was for his benefit. No, it would be to his benefit to know exactly what was going on in his life.

Nervousness spiked through her, settling deep. Kate smoothed a hand down her knee-length halter dress and took a deep breath as she stood beside her chair and waited for him to come in. Luc entered through the patio doors, closed them, set his phone on the coffee table and crossed to her.

"Smells great," he told her, offering a wide smile.

When he leaned down to kiss her cheek, Kate closed her eyes for the briefest of moments. Getting wrapped up in this entire scenario of playing house would only hurt her more. She wished more than anything that every bit of this scene playing out were true. Wished Luc would always look at her as if he loved her, as if he wanted to spend his life with her.

"My mother called," he told her after a long moment of silence. "She asked how everything was."

Kate moved the fish around on her plate, too nervous to actually eat. "I'm sure she's worried about you."

"She cares about me. I assume anyone who cares for me would be worried."

Kate's eyes slid up to his, a knot in her throat forming when she saw him staring back at her. "Yes. You have a great many people who love you."

"And what about you, Kate?" He held her gaze another moment before looking back to his plate. "Do you love me?"

Kate set her fork down, reached over to take his hand and squeezed. "I have so much in my heart for you, Luc."

When he said nothing, they finished eating, picked up the dishes and set them on the counter.

"Leave them," Luc told her, taking her hand. "Come with me."

When he led her toward the bedroom, Kate's heart started beating harder in her chest. She couldn't let him start kissing her, undressing her or even touching more than just her hand, because she'd melt instantly and not be able to follow through with her plan to spill her guts.

She trailed into the room after him. The bed in the center of the floor mocked her. Never again would they lie there in a tangle of arms and legs.

They never should have.

"Luc." She pulled her hand from his. "We can't."

He turned, quirking a brow. "Can't what?"

Kate shook her head, glancing away. She couldn't look him in the eyes. She didn't want to see his face when she revealed the truth.

"You can't make love to me?" He stepped closer, resting his hands on her shoulders. "Or you can't continue to play the role of doting fiancée? Because I have to tell you, you did a remarkable job of lying to my face."

Kate jerked her head up, meeting his cold, hard stare. All breath whooshed out of her lungs as fear gripped her heart like a vise.

"Apparently my real fiancée has been trying to get in touch with me," he went on, dropping his hands and stepping back as if he couldn't stand to touch Kate anymore. "After I heard my mother say that, the pieces started clicking into place."

Kate wrapped her arms around her waist. "You remember everything?"

"I know you're my assistant and you lied, manipulated and schemed to get into my bed." Luc laughed, the sound mocking. "Now I know why we never slept together before."

The pain in his voice sliced her heart open. Words died in her throat. Any defense she had was moot at this point.

"How far would you have gone, Kate? Would you have walked down the aisle and pretended to love me forever?"

She did love him. She'd chosen the absolute worst way to show him, but she truly did love the man. Kate pressed her lips together and remained still, waiting for the continuation of her punishment.

"Would you have gone so far as to have my kids?"

He took a step forward, but Kate squared her shoulders. She wasn't afraid of him and she wasn't going to turn and run, no matter how much she wanted to. Right now, he was entitled to lash out at her, and she had to take it.

"How could you do this to me?" His voice was low,

calm, cold. "Now I know why you cried after we had sex in the shower. Apparently, the guilt got to you, but only for a short time, because you were quick to get back in my bed."

Kate squeezed her arms tighter, as if to keep his hurtful words from seeping in. She glanced away, out the glass doors toward the sun, which had all but set.

"Look at me," he demanded. "You don't get to drift away. You started this and you're damn well going to face reality and give me the answers I want. Are you even going to say anything?"

Kate shook her head. "Anything I say won't change the fact that I lied to you, and you won't believe any defense I have."

Luc threw his arms out. "What was your motivation, Kate? Did you think I'd fall in love with you? Did you think you'd play with my mind for a bit?"

"No," she whispered through the tears clogging her throat. "Hurting you was the last thing I wanted to do."

"Oh, you didn't hurt me," he retorted, his face reddening. "I can't be hurt by someone I don't love. Didn't you know that? I'm furious I ever trusted you."

Kate nodded. "When we made love—"

"We didn't make love," he spat. Luc took a step closer, so close she could see the whiskey-colored flecks in his eyes. "We had sex. Meaningless sex that never should've happened."

Kate looked into his eyes, hoping to see a flicker of that emotion she'd seen during their days together, or when they'd been intimate. But all that stared back at her was hatred. Anything he thought he'd felt days ago, even hours ago, was false. The old Luc was back and harsher than ever.

"I'll call for someone to come pick me up," she told

him. "I'll be at the cottage until then. Anything I have here I can send for later."

Kate walked out of the room, surprised he didn't call her back so he could finish her off.

Mercifully, he let her go. She couldn't cry in front of him, didn't want him to think she was using tears as a defense. Her tears were a product of her own self-ishness. She'd lived it up for a few days, had had the man she loved in her arms and had even worn his ring.

Kate stepped out onto the patio and glanced down at the gem on her finger. Thunder rolled, lightning streaked in the not so distant sky as fat drops of rain pelted her.

"Kate," Luc called from behind her.

She froze.

"What the hell are you doing, just standing in the storm?"

Kate turned, blinking the rain out of her eyes. At this point she couldn't honestly tell what was rain and what were tears.

"Do you care?" she asked.

"I'm angry, but I don't want to see anyone struck by lightning."

Luc stood in the doorway, his broad frame filling the open space. The lights behind him flickered and then everything went black, save for the candles she'd lit on the dining room table and the fat pillar on the coffee table.

Cursing under his breath, Luc stepped back. "Get in here."

Slowly, Kate crossed the wet patio, hugging her mid-section against the cool drops. She brushed by him, shivering from the brief contact and cringing the second he stepped back and broke the touch.

"I just—"

"I'll be in my room." He cut her off with a wave of his hand as if she was nothing more than a nuisance. "Don't take this as a sign that I care. You can stay in here until the storm passes, and that's all."

Luc went to the dining room table, picked up a candle and walked away, leaving her shivering in the darkened living room. The pillar on the coffee table flickered, but she couldn't see much beyond the sofa. Kate sank down, pulling her feet up onto the cushion, hugging her knees to her chest.

Closing her eyes, she dropped her head forward and sighed. For the first time in her life she prayed the storm would stop. She had to get to her cottage, pack her things and call for someone to come and get her.

The hurt that had settled into this house was more than she could handle, and she didn't want to be here when Luc came out of his room. She didn't want to see that anger, that wounded look in his eyes again, knowing she'd put it there.

Whatever they'd had, be it their professional relationship or this fake engagement, she'd ruined any chance of ever having Luc in her life again. She'd taken what didn't belong to her, and she had no choice now but to live with the consequences.

Twelve

Luc must be insane. That was the only explanation for why he found himself crossing the path between the main house and the cottage so early in the morning. He hadn't slept all night. Every moment since his fall kept playing out in his mind like a movie, only he couldn't stop this one.

Kate's rigidity when he would initially touch her, her hesitancy to make love to him, why she was so adamant about him not buying her things at the market. The signs were there, but he'd assumed she was his fiancée, and she'd never said any differently. She'd had time, plenty of time, to tell him the truth. Even if the doctor hadn't given the order to not feed him any information, Luc was pretty sure she still would've kept up the charade.

Now that he'd had time to think, he'd fully processed how deeply her betrayal had sliced him. How could someone get so far into his life, work with him every single day, and manage to take advantage of him like that? Had he been that easy to manipulate? More important, how far would she have been willing to take that twisted game she'd played?

He wanted answers and he wanted them five minutes ago. He wasn't waiting another second to find out what the hell she'd been thinking to even contemplate getting away with such a potentially life-altering, monumental lie.

The anger raging inside him didn't stem just from her deception, but from the fact he'd fallen for her; making her betrayal even worse, Kate knew the emotional state he was in, just coming off a major breakup. Not only that, she knew he didn't date, much less sleep, with staff. How could she claim to care about him and then betray him in the next breath?

Even now that he knew everything, he still cared. He still ached for her, because with his old memories, he also had fresh ones. Memories he'd made with Kate, now tarnished by lies.

As Luc stepped into a clearing of lush plants, he glanced down to the dock. He froze when he spotted Kate standing by the water, two suitcases at her feet. She was not leaving without telling him why the hell she'd done this to him. She didn't get to escape that easily.

Marching toward the steps leading down to the beach, Luc had no clue what he'd say to her. She had plenty of explaining to do, but there was so much inside his mind, so much he wanted to say, he didn't even know where to start. He figured once he opened his mouth, things would start pouring out, most likely hurtful things. He couldn't care about her feelings just yet… if ever.

Kate jerked around as he approached. The dark circles beneath her eyes, the red rims, indicated she'd slept about as well as he had. The storm had lasted most of the night and he truly had no clue when she'd ended up leaving the main house. He'd closed the bedroom door, wanting to shut her out. Unfortunately, his bedroom was filled with visions of Kate.

The shower, the bed, her pair of flip-flops by the closet door, her robe draped across the foot of the bed. She was everywhere, and she'd wedged herself so intimately into his life, as no other woman had.

She'd had so much control over the situation and she'd used that power to consume him. Now he had to figure out how the hell to get out from under her spell, because even seeing her right now, with all his bubbling rage, he found his body still responded to her.

Damn it. How could he still want her? Anything that had happened between them was dead to him. He couldn't think back on those times, because just like this "engagement," they meant nothing.

Her eyes widened as he came to stand within inches of her. "I'm waiting for a boat. My father is sending one of the guards to pick me up."

"Why?" Luc asked, clenching his fists at his sides. "Before you leave, tell me why you lied to me."

Her head tipped slightly as she studied him. "Would it matter?"

Strands of her long, dark hair had slipped loose from her knot and were dancing about her shoulders. She had on another of those little strapless sundresses, this one black. Appropriately matching the color of his mood.

"Maybe not, but I deserve to know why you would betray my trust and think it was okay."

Dark eyes held his. Part of him wanted to admire her

for not backing away, not playing the victim or defending herself. The other part wished she'd defend herself and say something, so they could argue about it and get everything out in the open. He needed a good outlet, someone to yell at, and the perfect target stood directly in front of him.

"I was shocked at first that you thought I was your fiancée," she told him, her pink tongue darting out to lick her lips. She shoved a wayward strand of hair behind her ear and shrugged. "Then I wanted to see what the doctor would say before I told you otherwise. He said not to give you any information, so I didn't. I didn't want to lie to you, Luc. I was in a tough spot and everything blew out of my control before I knew what was happening. I tried to keep my distance, but once we had sex, I wanted more. I took what I shouldn't have. Nothing I can say can change that fact, but I am sorry I hurt you."

Luc propped his hands on his hips, waiting to hear more, but she remained silent and continued to hold his gaze. "There has to be another reason, a deeper motivation than you simply being afraid to tell me."

Kate's eyes darted away as she turned her back to him and focused on the water again. Not a boat in sight. He still had time to get answers from her before she left.

"My reasons are irrelevant."

He almost didn't hear her whispered answer over the ocean breeze. With her back to him, Luc wasn't sure what was worse, looking her in the eyes or looking at that exposed, creamy neck he could practically taste. He would never taste that skin again.

He cursed beneath his breath, raked a hand down his face and sighed. "What were you trying to gain?" he demanded. "I'm giving you the opportunity to say something here, Kate. Tell me why I shouldn't fire you, why I shouldn't remove you from every aspect of my life."

The low hum of a motor jerked his attention in the direction of the royal yacht moving toward them. Kate said nothing as she turned, picking up her suitcases.

Here he was gearing up for a good fight, and she couldn't even afford him that? Did she feel nothing at all? How had he misread her all these years?

If she wasn't going to talk now, then fine. He wasn't done with her, but if she needed to go, he'd let her. She could stew and worry back in Ilha Beleza. Luc actually wanted her uncomfortable, contemplating his next move. She deserved to be miserable, and he had to steel himself against any remorse.

His mother had always taught him to respect women, which he did, but right now that didn't mean he had to make her life all rainbows and sunshine, either.

"Go back to the palace," he told her, hating how she refused to look at him. "I'll be home in a few days and we'll add on to that schedule we finalized the other night."

Kate threw him a glance over her shoulder. "What?"

Luc stepped around her, blocking her view of the incoming boat. He waited until her eyes locked onto his. "You're not quitting. You're going to be with me until I know what game you're playing. And don't try to get sneaky once you're back. I have eyes and ears everywhere."

Her chin tipped up in defiance...a quality he'd once admired when she was speaking with the media or other pushy individuals. "I think it's best if I resign."

Luc gripped her shoulders, cursing himself for having a weakness where she was concerned, considering all she'd done. "I don't care what you think is best.

You're mine until I say otherwise. You started this game, Kate. You're going to see it through to the end."

Pushing away from her, he stalked toward the main house. Not once did he consider glancing back. He was finished looking over his shoulder to see if anyone was stabbing him in the back or betraying him. From here on out, he was regaining control, and he was damn well going to come out on top.

Luc stared at the area he used to call his kitchen. If this royalty thing didn't work out, he was seriously getting a job with a contractor. Demolishing things was an excellent outlet for his anger.

Wiping his forearm across his forehead, he sank down onto a dining room chair and surveyed his destruction. The cabinets were torn out; the countertop lay beneath the rubble. He'd pulled the fridge out enough that he could get to the food, but other than that, he'd completely torn up the space.

Kate had been gone a week. Two weeks had passed since he'd arrived here, and he was heading home tomorrow. In these past seven days alone, he'd had more than enough time to reflect on everything, and he still had no clue what he was going to do once he saw her again.

He'd had to sleep in the guest room on a lumpy old mattress because he couldn't lie in his master suite without smelling her, seeing her...feeling her at his side. The shower he'd so loved when the renovations started was now tainted, because all he could see was Kate's wet body as he claimed her with the false knowledge they were a real couple. They'd been damn good together, but he would never, ever admit that to her or anybody else.

Luc's cell chimed. He thought about ignoring it, but figured he'd at least see who wanted to talk to him.

Crossing the open room, he glanced at his phone on the coffee table. Mikos, his best friend.

Considering he had called Mikos three days ago and spilled his guts like some whiny high school girl with sad love songs playing in the background, Luc assumed his friend was calling to check on him.

"Hey, man," he answered with a sigh.

"You still sound like hell."

Luc laughed, sinking onto the sofa, resting his elbow on the arm. "Yeah, well, I feel like it. What's up?"

"Just checking in."

"Shouldn't you be planning the wedding of the century?" Luc asked, feeling a slight pang of envy.

Envy? Why the hell would he be envious? Sure, he needed to be married because of the throne, but he didn't want to be tied to one woman. No, Mikos had found the perfect woman for him, and Luc was happy for both of them.

There was no perfect woman for Luc. Hadn't he proved that by getting too close to two very convincing liars?

"The wedding is planned down to the last petal and place card," Mikos stated. "Are you still in?"

Luc was supposed to stand up with Mikos, right next to Mikos's brother, Stefan. An honor Luc wasn't letting Kate's untimely backstabbing steal from him.

"I'm in. I'm not letting my disaster ruin your day."

"Have you talked to Kate?"

Luc closed his eyes. Even hearing her name elicited a mixture of feelings, a myriad of emotions. Beyond the hurt, the anger and the bitterness there was still that underlying fact that he wanted the hell out of her. How twisted was that?

"No. I'm heading back tomorrow," Luc answered.

"What are you going to do?"

"I have no clue, man."

Mikos sighed. "Want my advice?"

"You're going to give it anyway, so why ask?"

"I am," Mikos agreed with a laugh. "Figure out why she lied. You told me once you had a thing for her. Maybe she was acting on her own feelings and taking a cue from yours before the accident."

"Are you defending her actions?" The last thing Luc wanted to hear was a justifiable cause. Damn it, he wanted to be angry, wanted to place all the blame on her.

"Hell, no. I'm saying love is a strong emotion."

"You're too blinded by this wedding," Luc replied. "Kate doesn't love me. You don't lie and scheme with those you love, no matter the circumstances."

"I did to Darcy," Mikos reminded him. "She had no idea who I was, and I was totally in love with her. I nearly lost her, but she forgave me. You know how things can get mixed up, Luc."

Luc recalled that time when Mikos's nanny had first been hired. She'd had no clue Mikos was a widowed prince. The two had fallen in love before Mikos could fully explain the truth.

"Our situations are completely different," Luc muttered. "I'm not forgiving her. No matter what."

"Just make sure you really think this through before you go off on her once you get home," Mikos warned. "What she did was wrong, no doubt about it. But she's not like Alana. I know that's something you'll never forget or get over, but Alana had an ulterior motive from the start. You've known Kate for years and she's never once done you wrong."

Luc finished the call, unable to think of anything else but the truth Mikos had laid out before him. No, Kate had never deceived him in any way before. She'd been the best assistant he'd ever had. To be honest, the only reason he hadn't pursued her before was because of their working relationship and possible repercussions to his ascension to the throne. With the mess he'd gotten himself into lately, it would be a miracle if the press didn't rip his family's reputation to shreds if the truth came out.

Once he returned to Ilha Beleza, he and Kate would have a one-on-one chat, now that they'd both had time to absorb all that had happened. They needed to talk. He couldn't keep her around if he didn't trust her. And that was the problem. When it came to his professional life, he trusted no one else.

Unfortunately, when it came to his personal life, he didn't trust her one bit...but that didn't stop him from wanting her. Even this week apart hadn't dimmed his attraction toward her. Which begged the question: What the hell was going to happen once he got home? And would he be able to control himself?

Thirteen

His desk was exactly how he always kept it—neat, tidy and organized, with his schedule in hard copies just as he wanted it. He knew there would also be emails on his computer with the same information.

Kate had kept up her end of the bargain and continued working just as if she hadn't torn their entire lives to shreds. He didn't know whether to be relieved or angry that she was still here, still within reaching distance... not that he was going to reach out to her. He had more pride than that.

Luc flipped through the papers, even though he'd looked through his email earlier and knew what he had coming up. Mikos's wedding was only two weeks away, and other than that, there were a handful of meetings and social events at which he was expected to make an appearance. He'd been knocked down so many times in the past few months he didn't know if he had the energy to put forth for anyone outside his immediate family and staff. He was so exhausted, spent and depleted from trying to perform damage control on his personal life, there was no way he could keep up with his royal obligations, too.

Thankfully, from the looks of his schedule, Kate had helped him dodge any media interviews over the next few months. For that he was grateful, but not enough to seek her out and thank her. He wasn't ready to thank her for anything...and he might never be.

"Oh, sweetheart. You're back."

Luc glanced toward the high, arched doorway as his mother breezed in. The woman possessed more elegance and grace than anyone he'd ever known. With her polished style and loving grin, she made the perfect queen, but her reign was soon coming to an end. Well, it would be if he managed to find a way to secure his title before his birthday, and without a wife.

Luc crossed the room and relished her embrace. Even though he'd always been close with his parents, he didn't have it in him to discuss all the ways he was struggling right now.

"How are you?" she asked, pulling back to assess him. Clutching his arms, she studied his face. "No more symptoms? You remember everything now?"

Luc nodded. "I'm perfectly fine."

She held on to him another moment, then broke the contact. "We need to talk."

He crossed his arms as his mother shut the double doors, giving them complete privacy.

"Have you seen Kate since you've been back?" she asked.

Luc shook his head. "No."

"Darling, she told me what happened." His mother

reached out, took one of his hands in hers and squeezed. "I'm sure she left out some details, but I know you believed she was your fiancée, and she went along with it."

Luc gritted his teeth. Seriously? Kate went to his mom?

"I wished I'd learned this from you," she went on. "I can't imagine how angry you must be, and I know you're feeling betrayed—"

"Don't defend her," Luc growled. "I'm not near that point."

"I'm not defending her actions." His mother smiled, tipping her head. "I just want you to really think about how you're going to handle this. Kate is a wonderful woman and I've always been so fond of her. I know we have a rule about remaining distant from employees, but she and her parents have been around so long, they're like family."

His feelings for Kate were far from family-like, and he sure as hell hadn't been feeling brotherly in that shower.

"I will admit I'm surprised you didn't fire her," his mother added. "She's good for you, Luc. She's the best assistant you've ever had. I'm proud of you for not blowing up."

"It was tempting."

Temptation. The word seemed to go hand in hand with Kate's name.

"I still don't know what to do, but for now, she's going to be working for me like always. I don't have time to find a new assistant, and I sure as hell don't want to have to get to know someone new. I've got enough of a mess to deal with."

"We do need to figure out what's going to happen on your birthday." His mother pursed her lips, as if in deep thought. "Your father would change the law if he could, but the truth is, we never dreamed…"

Luc laughed, the sound void of all humor. "I know. You never thought a child of yours would still be single at thirty-five. It's okay to say it."

She squeezed his arm. "We'll figure something out. We have to."

Luc nodded, unable to speak past the lump of worry in his throat. Failure was not an option. Ever. He was the next leader, for crying out loud. Why couldn't he figure out a way around this ridiculous issue?

"I'll let you get settled back in, then." His mother reached up, kissed him on the cheek. "Glad you're back home and safe. And I'm glad you didn't fire Kate. She means more to this family than you may realize."

What did that mean? Did his mother actually think he and Kate…

No. That was ridiculous. As torn as he was, he couldn't entertain the idea that Kate could remain in his life as anything other than his assistant…and even that role was still up in the air. He'd have to worry about that later. At this point, time was against him, and finding another assistant before finding a wife—or before the coronation—was impossible.

Once he was alone again, Luc turned and went to his desk. Bracing his palms on its glossy top, he leaned forward and closed his eyes. He would do a great job ruling this country, as his father had before him. Luc just needed a chance to prove he could do so without a wife.

The echo of soft footsteps hit him and he knew instantly who would be behind him. He didn't turn, though. He wasn't quite ready to take in the sight of Kate with all her beauty and sexiness.

The click of the heels stopped, Luc's heart beat faster

than he liked. Damn it, he hadn't even turned to look at her, hadn't said a word, yet she had already sent his body into overdrive.

"I'll come back."

Her soft words washed over him as he turned to face her.

"No." He spoke to her retreating back, and she froze in the doorway. "Come in and close the door."

She stood still so long, he thought for sure she wasn't going to stay. After a moment, she stepped back, closed the door and whipped around to face him.

Luc hadn't thought it possible, but he still found her breathtakingly gorgeous and arousing. Seeing Kate in a dark blue suit, with a fitted jacket that hugged her waist and accentuated her breasts, and her snug skirt made it hard for him to form words right now. As her heels clicked across the floor, his eyes were drawn to her open-toed, animal-print pumps. Damn, she looked like a woman who was ready to be stripped and laid out on his desk.

What was worse, now that he'd had her wrapped all around him, he knew exactly how amazing they were together. Why was he paying a penance in all this? He was the victim.

She stopped well out of his reach, clasped her hands in front of her and met his gaze. "I didn't know you were back," she said. "I was just coming in to make sure your computer was ready to go when you needed it."

Luc tore his gaze from her painted red lips and glanced at his desk. He hadn't even noticed the new computer. Hell, he hadn't even asked for one. Once again, she stayed on top of things and kept his life running smoothly.

"Where's my old one?" he asked.

"All of the palace computers have been upgraded, and they put yours in while you were gone. I made sure the security on yours was set up the same as your old one, and I also made sure your old files were transferred. Everything is on there under the same names, just how they always were."

When he glanced back at her, there wasn't a hint of any emotion on her face. Not a twinge of a smile, no dark circles under her eyes to indicate she'd been losing sleep. Absolutely nothing.

Which pissed him off even more.

"Is this how it's going to be?" he asked, gritting his teeth. "With you pretending you didn't change the dynamics between us?"

Kate blinked, pulled in a deep breath and shook her head. "I don't know what you want from me. I can't erase what happened, yet you still want me to work for you, so I'm doing what I can under the circumstances. I can't tell you what you want to know, because—"

She spun around. Luc waited for her to finish, but she kept her back to him as silence settled heavily between them. There was no easy way, no secret formula for them to get beyond this. He wasn't all that convinced they could move on, despite what his mother and Mikos had said during their pep talks.

"Because why?" he pressed, when she remained quiet. "Why can't you tell me your reasons? I'm ready to hear it. I *need* to hear it, Kate."

Still nothing. Luc stepped forward, closing the space between them. "Damn it, I deserve more than your silence. You can't hide like this. You don't get that right. Tell me what prompted you to not only lie, but keep up the charade and play me so perfectly that you ended up in my bed."

"Don't," she whispered. "Don't make me say it."

Luc grabbed her arm, spun her around and forced himself to hold her watery gaze. "I refuse to let you out of this scot-free."

Squaring her shoulders, tipping her chin up and swiping a hand beneath her eye as one lone tear streaked out, Kate nodded. "Fine. You want to know why I did it? Why I lied to you so easily? Besides the doctor's orders of not saying anything more, besides the fact that the deception just got out of control, I knew it was the only time in my life you'd ever look at me like you cared for me. Like you actually wanted me. I knew it was wrong. I never justified my actions, and I won't defend them, because there's no way to make any of it okay. But don't make me tell you more. I can't, Luc."

Her voice cracked on his name. Luc kept his hand on her arm as he took a half step closer, nearly towering over her. "You can," he murmured. "Tell me the rest. Now."

He was so torn between arousal and anger. He'd always heard there was a fine line between hatred and passion. No truer words were ever spoken.

"I fell in love with you," she whispered, her eyes locking onto his. "Is that what you wanted to hear? Do you hate me so much that humiliating me is the only way to make yourself get past the anger? Well, now you know. I've bared my soul to you, Luc. You know about my adoption, which few people do. You know my secret fantasies—you're the only one in that category—and that I'm in love with a man who'd rather belittle me than ever forgive me, let alone love me back. My fault, I know, but that doesn't stop the hurt."

A viselike grip squeezed his heart at her declaration. Why did he feel anything akin to sympathy toward her? She'd done every bit of this to herself, pulling him along for the ride.

"You don't love me." He dropped his hand and stepped back. "You don't lie to someone and manipulate them, taking advantage of their weaknesses, when you love them."

"I never lied to you before this and I won't lie to you again," she vowed, crossing her arms over her chest. "So when I tell you I love you, I'm being honest. I know my word means nothing to you, and I know I went about everything the wrong way. There is no excuse for my behavior, so I'm not going to stand here and try to make one."

Luc watched as she pulled herself together, patting her damp cheeks, smoothing her hair behind her shoulders and standing tall.

Even through all this, she remained strong. He wanted to hate her, because that would be so much easier than to stand here and be torn in two. She'd betrayed the trust they had built, yet at the same time she had tried to keep her distance. He'd been the one to pursue the intimacy. He could look at this situation from so many angles, but none of them gave him the answer or made things any easier.

"You have every right to fire me—I deserve it. But if you insist on keeping me, I think it's best if we keep our relationship professional and try to move on. That means no rehashing the mistakes I made. I can't have you throwing them in my face."

The longer she spoke, the stronger her voice got. The woman who'd emotionally professed her love for him just moments earlier had transformed back into the businesslike assistant he'd always known. Who was the real Kate?

Was she the loving, passionate woman back at the beach house? Was she the take-charge assistant, or was she the conniving woman who'd ruthlessly insinuated herself into his life when he'd been weak?

"I agree that from here on out, we'll keep our relationship strictly professional."

Luc prayed like hell he was telling the truth. He needed to keep his head on straight, focus on securing the title and not think about how much he'd fallen for his assistant.

Well, that plan to keep things professional was about to get blown apart.

Kate closed her eyes, gripped the stick and willed the results to be different.

Peeking through one eyelid, she still saw the two pink lines glaring back at her. If they had been on a billboard or neon sign they couldn't have been any more eye-catching… She couldn't look anywhere else.

And no matter how long she stared at it, the results were still going to be the same. Positive.

Something between a moan and a cry escaped her as she came to her feet. Staring at herself in the vanity mirror, Kate didn't know what she expected to see. She didn't look any different, but in the past three minutes the course of her entire life had been altered.

Now what should she do? She was pregnant with Luc's baby and the man practically loathed her, unless she was writing a speech for him or running interference for some engagement he didn't want to attend.

There was no getting around this. She'd been on the pill since she was a teen, to keep her cycle regular, but they hadn't used a condom the times they'd been intimate, and birth control wasn't fail-safe…obviously.

There was only one answer. She'd promised Luc she'd never lie to him again, and she certainly wasn't going to start off by keeping this baby a secret.

Laying the test stick on the back of the vanity, Kate washed her hands and stepped out of the restroom. She wanted to find Luc now. This couldn't wait, because the nerves in her stomach were threatening to overtake her. She had to find him.

At this point in the day, she honestly had no idea what he was doing, but she did know he was working from home. If she stopped to think, she could figure out his schedule—she had created it. But her mind wasn't in work mode right now and she couldn't process anything other than the fact she was having a baby with a man she loved…a man who could hardly look at her. She was on the verge of freaking out.

Her lies had not only killed the trust Luc had for her, now the whirlwind of secrets had formed a new life…literally.

Kate's hand slid over her stomach as she made her way out of her office and into the wide hallway. She smiled as she passed one of the maids, but her smile faded the second she reached Luc's office door. In just moments, both their lives and the future of this country would be changed forever.

She was carrying an heir.

Kate rested her forehead against the smooth wood and closed her eyes. The sooner she told Luc, the sooner they could start figuring out what to do. Summoning all the strength she possessed, she tapped on his office door, cursing her shaking hands. She heard familiar voices on the other side. Apparently, he was having a private meeting with his parents. Still, this couldn't wait.

Yes, they were the king and queen. Yes, Kate was being rude by interrupting. But she didn't care.

Fisting her hand, she knocked louder and longer, until the door jerked open to an angry-looking Luc. His jaw clenched, his lips thinned, and once he saw her, his eyes narrowed.

"Kate? We're in the middle of something."

Pushing by him, she offered a shaky smile to his parents, who sat with their eyes locked on her. "I'm sorry, but this can't wait."

Ana Silva rose to her feet and crossed the room. Kate swallowed as her heart started beating faster. She was going to be sick. The overwhelming urge to pass out or throw up all over the Persian rug had nothing to do with the pregnancy.

"Darling, you're trembling," Ana said. "Come, sit down."

"We're in the middle of something," Luc repeated.

Luc's father stood, gesturing toward the chair he'd just vacated. "Here, Kate."

Luc muttered a string of Portuguese slang.

"I'm sorry," Kate muttered. "I didn't mean to cause a scene. I just need a few minutes with Luc."

His parents exchanged a look and Kate noticed Luc standing off to the side, arms crossed, jaw still clenched. He wasn't happy. Too bad she was about to drop another bomb on his life. Would he be even angrier at her? Most likely, but hiding the pregnancy wasn't an option.

Kate closed her eyes as she rested her elbows on her knees and dropped her head into her hands. Luc's parents muttered something to him and moments later Kate heard the office door click shut.

"What the hell is this all about?" Luc demanded.

Kate pushed her hair away from her face as she looked up. He was leaning against the edge of his desk, ankles crossed, palms resting on either side of his slim hips. Wearing dark designer jeans and a fitted black T-shirt, he didn't look like a member of the royal family, but he still exuded power. It was the stare, the unyielding body language, that told her she needed to get on with her speech...one she hadn't rehearsed at all.

"I..." Kate shook her head, came to her feet. No way could she remain still; her body was too shaky, too wound up to stay seated.

"Just say it."

Luc's harsh words cut through her. Kate stopped pacing, turned and gazed at him. "I'm pregnant."

He stared at her for several moments without saying a word. Then suddenly, he burst out laughing, and straightened.

"Nice try, Kate." His expression sobered. "That's already been used on me."

"What?"

His words took a moment to sink in. He didn't believe her. Of course he wouldn't. Why should he? He'd been played for a fool by his ex-fiancée, who tried the pregnancy trap, and Kate had also lied to him.

"Luc, I'm not lying," she reiterated. "I have the test in my office bathroom. I need to call Dr. Couchot to confirm with a blood test, though."

Something dark clouded Luc's eyes. "You did this on purpose."

Fury rose to the surface, pushing through the nerves. No matter how much she loved him, no matter how much she wished he would see her as a woman worthy of his love and trust, Kate refused to stand here and be degraded and blamed for something they'd both taken part in.

"I think it was you who came to me," she retorted,

crossing her arms over her chest. "You think I wanted a child with a man who doesn't love me? I made a mistake by lying to you, but I'm not pathetic and I'm not trying to trap you. I promised I would always be honest with you, and I just found out about this myself ten minutes ago. So lose the ego. I don't want to snag you that much."

Kate turned to go and managed to get across the room with her hand on the doorknob before Luc grabbed her arm and spun her back around. Leaning flat against the door, trapped between the wood and Luc's hard body, she stared up into those eyes that could make a woman forget all her problems...almost. Even the great Prince Lucas Silva wasn't that powerful.

"You think you can drop that bomb and then just walk out?" he demanded. "We're not done here."

"We both need to process this before we say anything we might regret." Though they'd already said plenty to cause damaging scars. "I just need... I need to think this through, Luc."

His eyes widened. "What's there to think through? You're having my child. I will be part of his or her life."

A sliver of relief coursed through her. "I would never deny you the chance to be with your child."

Tears welled up, the familiar burn in her throat formed and Kate cursed herself. She absolutely hated crying, hated the predicament she was in, but hated even more that she was pulling in an innocent child.

"I'm scared," she whispered, closing her eyes.

She jerked when Luc's hand slid over her cheek. Focusing back on him, she saw something in his eyes she hadn't expected...fear. Obviously, she wasn't the only one with insecurities.

"No matter what happened prior to this moment,

I won't leave you alone with a baby." He dropped his hand, but didn't step back. "Our baby."

When he stood so close, smelling so amazingly familiar and feeling so sexy against her, Kate couldn't think straight. She wished she didn't still want him, wished she'd never lied to him to begin with. And she truly wished something as beautiful as creating a life with the man she loved hadn't been tainted because of her lies.

"I don't want our baby to suffer from my actions," she told him. "I want to be able to work with you on this, and I know the timing—"

She cut herself off with a sad laugh. "Sorry. There would be no good timing," she corrected. "I just meant with the throne, your birthday and all of that on your mind, I didn't mean to add to your stress, but you needed to know."

When he said nothing, Kate carefully turned. There was no way to avoid rubbing up against him, because he'd barely moved since he'd trapped her against the door.

Luc's hands came up to cup her shoulders as he moved in behind her.

"Who are you, Kate?" he whispered.

Her head dropped against the wood as she tried to ignore all of the ways her body responded to his. Tried and failed miserably.

"Are you the efficient assistant? The woman who stands up for me to the public? Are you the woman who lied to me for selfish reasons? Or are you the woman who claims to love me and who's now carrying my child?"

Drawing in a shaky breath, Kate glanced over her shoulder just enough to catch his gaze. "I'm all of them."

"Part of me hates you for what you did." Luc's eyes darted down to her lips. "I wish I still didn't want you so damn much."

Breath caught in Kate's throat as Luc pushed away and stalked back to his desk. He kept his back to her, as if that revelation had cost him dearly. She had no doubt he hadn't meant to let that slip, and as much as she wanted to revel in his obvious discomfort over the fact that he wanted her, Kate had to put this baby first, above all else.

Even the fact that her own heart was still beating for only one man.

Fourteen

He hadn't planned on taking Kate to Greece for his best friend's wedding, but once she had opened her heart to him and bared her soul, Luc wasn't able to deny the fact that he still wanted her.

Plans were taking root in his mind and he was going to have to take action. Perhaps he could have Kate, the crown and his child without ever putting his heart on the line where she was concerned. Surely she'd stay for the sake of their child. Why not make it official, so he could keep the title that was rightfully his?

But if he wanted to sway her into marriage, he needed to start convincing her, or she'd never say yes.

No, he hadn't forgiven her for lying, but she was pregnant, confirmed by Dr. Couchot, and Luc knew the child was his. The plan forming in his mind was anything but nice, but he couldn't back down. Too much was at stake.

Luc glanced across the aisle to where Kate had re-clined her seat and was curled onto her side, with her hand beneath her cheek. She'd been exhausted when they'd left that morning, and he'd nearly told her to stay behind, but he knew she was just as stubborn as him and wouldn't listen. Either the baby was making her more tired than usual or she wasn't sleeping because of the stress. Knowing her, it was probably both.

He'd cursed himself every which way after she'd left his office a few days ago. He'd hated how his heart had flipped when she'd whispered her fears. Damn it, he didn't want his heart to be affected by this woman. There was no space in his life for such things. He had a title to secure, and now he had an heir to think about. Kate couldn't fall under the category of things he cared about, because if he allowed that, then she would have the upper hand. Wanting her physically was difficult enough to have to deal with each time she was near.

His mind kept wandering back to how right it had felt when they'd been playing house. He'd gladly dis-missed his family's rule about fraternizing with staff. He would have done anything for her. He'd never felt so connected to a woman in all his life.

Kate embodied sex appeal, that was a given. It had been what had drawn him to her when she'd first come to work for him. He vaguely recalled the little girl, and later on the teen, who used to hang around the palace with her parents.

Then when the time came that he'd needed an assis-tant and Kate had been recommended, he'd jumped at the chance, because her family knew his so well and he knew she'd be a trustworthy candidate. Plus her refer-ences and academics had been superb.

Yet somehow, over the course of a professional relationship that had started out with an attraction, and involved his messy engagement to another woman, Luc's life had spiraled spectacularly out of control.

The irony that he'd gone from a fiancée with a fake pregnancy to a poser fiancée with a real pregnancy was not lost on him. He was a walking tabloid and fodder for the press. Thankfully, Kate was in charge of press releases, and no doubt she'd come up with something amazingly brilliant once they were ready to go public.

Kate stirred in her sleep, letting out a soft moan. The simple sound hit his gut with a swift punch of lust he couldn't ignore. He'd heard those moans in his ear as she'd wrapped her body around his. He'd felt the whisper of breath on his skin that accompanied her sighs.

But no matter how compatible they were in the bedroom, no matter how much he still ached for her on a level he'd never admit aloud, Luc wouldn't, couldn't, allow himself to be pulled into whatever spell Kate had over him.

Even if he would let his guard down and shove the royal rule aside and see a staff member personally, Kate had killed any chance of him ever trusting her fully. So she could sit across from him and make all the noises she wanted; he was ignoring them.

Too bad his body hadn't received that memo, because certain parts of him couldn't forget the intimacy they'd shared.

Luc needed to focus on the brilliant plot he'd started forming. Would she be angry when he approached her with the solution? Yes. Did he care? No. He was plenty angry still, but he wanted her, wanted the crown and refused to allow his heart to become vulnerable again.

The phone near Luc's seat rang and the pilot informed him they'd be landing within a half hour. Once

Luc hung up, he crossed the space and sank down in the plush white leather chair next to Kate. He hated waking her up. Not that he was worried about disturbing her sleep; he was more concerned with the fact he'd have to touch her, have to see her blinking back to reality as she sat there, looking all rumpled and sexy.

As if she was ever *not* appealing. But he couldn't be blinded by lust and sexual chemistry. He didn't need a bed partner, no matter what his body told him. Making love with her was how he'd gotten entangled in this web to begin with.

"Kate."

He purposely said her name loudly, so she'd wake without him having to lay a hand on her. She let out a soft snore and Luc gritted his teeth and called her name again.

Still nothing.

Who was he kidding? It didn't matter if he touched her or not. He wanted her, his body responded to her as it had to no other woman and she was carrying his child. As if he needed another reason to be physically pulled toward her. Knowing she was carrying his child was beyond sexy. There was something so primal about knowing Kate sat there with their baby safely inside her body.

Even when Alana had said she was expecting, Luc hadn't felt this much of a tug on his heart. He'd had an instant protective instinct toward the child, but he'd never felt a bond with Alana.

Damn it, he couldn't afford a tug on his heart or some invisible bond. Kate wasn't trustworthy. Regardless, he didn't need her trust for his plan to work. He didn't need anything from her, because he wouldn't take no for an answer.

Marrying Kate was the only solution. As much as he hated to give in to his country's archaic rule, it was the only way to come out of this situation on top. Some marriages were based on far less than sexual chemistry and they worked just fine.

The fact remained that he still wanted her something fierce. He wanted her with an intensity that scared him, but he had to risk his heart, his sanity, in order to get what he wanted.

Luc reached around, pulled on her seat belt and fastened it with a click. Just as he was about to move away and fasten his own, Kate jerked awake. Sleepy eyes locked onto his and he realized his mistake. He'd leaned in too close, so close he was only inches from her face, and his hand hovered over her abdomen.

"What are you doing?" she asked, her voice husky from sleep.

"Preparing you for landing."

Why hadn't he eased back, and why was he staring at her lips?

"You can't look at me like that, Luc," she whispered. "You don't even like me."

Something clenched in his gut. Something harsher, more intense than lust.

He was a damn *tolo*. Fool. That was the only explanation for having these reactions after what she'd done to him. He needed to focus on the plan, the throne, the baby. Everything else—including his lustful feelings—would have to be put aside.

"I don't trust you," he countered. "There's a difference."

Those heavy lids shielded her dark eyes for a moment as she stared down to where his hands lay on her stomach.

"I didn't trap you," she whispered as her eyes drifted back up to his. "No matter what you think of me, I'd never do that to you or an innocent child."

Luc swallowed as her hand settled over his. There was so much emotion in her eyes, so much he was too afraid to identify, because if he did, he'd start feeling more for her, and he refused to be played like a *fantouche*, a puppet, for a third time.

Pride and ego fueled his decisions. Power and control ran a close second. And all those things combined would get him everything he'd ever wanted...everything he was entitled to.

Luc shifted to sit up, but didn't remove his hand, and for some asinine reason he didn't break eye contact, either. Obviously, he was a glutton for punishment.

"I want you to move into the palace."

Of course, he had bigger plans, but he had to ease her into this. She wasn't the only one skilled at manipulation.

"I'm not sure that's a good idea."

She removed her hand from his, a silent plea for him to move, so he pulled back. The first slight dip in the plane's decent reminded Luc he hadn't fastened his seat belt because he'd been worried for her. He quickly buckled it, then turned his attention back to Kate.

"Why not?" he asked. "Moving into the palace is the ideal solution. We'll be sharing responsibilities. I know we'll hire a nanny, but I plan on being a hands-on dad."

Kate shoved her hair away from her face. A thin sleep mark ran down her cheek. It made her seem so vulnerable, and it was all he could do not to touch her again. "What will happen when you want to actually marry someone? Are you going to explain to your bride that your baby mama is living there, too?"

Luc laughed. "That's a pretty crass way to put it."

Kate shrugged, lacing her fingers together as she glanced out the window. "I'm not sugarcoating this situation and neither should you."

Luc didn't say anything else. He would sway her with his actions, not his words. She would come to see that living with him, ultimately marrying him, would be the best way to approach their predicament. And when they married, she would be sleeping in his bed again. He'd make sure of it.

Now he just needed to get his hormones under control, because he was physically aching for her. Being near her now that he'd had her was pure hell. The woman was made for him. Nobody had ever matched him in the bedroom—or shower—the way she did.

Yet Kate was so much more than a sex partner. He'd discovered an emptiness in him now that they were back to keeping things professional. No matter the circumstances surrounding the false engagement, Luc couldn't help but think back and realize those days spent on the island were some of the happiest of his life.

Kate had been to many royal events over the past year as an official employee of the Silva family. Before that, she'd seen enough to know that royalty never did anything halfway, especially when it came to weddings.

The ceremony uniting Darcy and Mikos Alexander had taken place earlier in the day, and now only the couple's closest family and guests, of which there appeared to be several hundred, remained for the reception.

No expense had been spared for the event taking place both in the ballroom and out in the courtyard at the palace on Galini Isle, off the coast of Greece. Every stationary item was draped with something crystal, shimmering or sheer.

As she watched the bride and groom dance, Kate couldn't help but smile. Mikos had lost his first wife suddenly, leaving him to care for their infant daughter alone. Needing a break, he'd gone to Los Angeles to get away and think. He'd hired Darcy to be his daughter's nanny, and before long the two had fallen in love...even though Mikos had slightly deceived Darcy, because she'd had no idea he was royalty. Of course, none of that had made it to the press, but Kate knew the whole story from Luc.

Luc and Mikos had been best friends forever. Kate was quite familiar with Mikos and his brother, Stefan, who was also in attendance, with his stunning wife, Victoria.

Even if the crystal chandeliers, flawless ice sculptures, millions of clear twinkling lights and yards upon yards of sheer draping hadn't screamed elegance and beauty, the gorgeous people milling about certainly would have.

This was definitely one of those times she was thankful her mother was the royal seamstress. By the time Luc had sprung the trip on her, Kate hadn't had time to go shopping. So her mom had taken an old gown and made enough modifications to transform it into something lovely and totally unique. What had once been a simple, fitted silver dress was now unrecognizable. The sleeves had been removed and the top had been cut into a sweetheart neckline to give the allure of sexiness with a slight show of cleavage. Her mother had then had the brilliant idea of taking strands of clear beads and sewing them so they would drape across Kate's arms, as if her straps had fallen and settled just above her biceps.

Kate actually felt beautiful in this dress, and judging from the way Luc had stared at her without saying a word when he'd come to get her for the wedding, she had to assume he thought she looked nice, as well.

She still couldn't get the image out of her mind of him waking her for the landing. He'd been so close, staring at her as if he wanted to touch her, kiss her. Their chemistry wasn't in question, that was obvious, but he clearly battled whether or not to act on it.

Maybe their time apart would have him coming around, to see that she truly wasn't aiming for the crown. She sure as hell wasn't Alana.

Nervously glancing around the room, Kate toyed with the amethyst pendant that hung just above her breasts. She hadn't worn the ring Luc had bought her; that would've just felt wrong. She'd actually placed it in his desk drawer days ago, though she had no clue if he'd found it.

Since Luc had started his best-man duties, she'd pretty much been on her own. That was fine, actually. The more she was around Luc, the harder she was finding it to face the reality that while she was having his baby, he'd never see her as more than a speech writer who happened to be giving him an heir.

Once the evening wound down, perhaps they could talk. She held out hope that he would remember the woman she was before his accident, not the liar she'd turned into for a few short days.

"Champagne, ma'am?"

The waiter, balancing a tray full of flutes of the bubbly drink, smiled at her. Kate shook her head.

"No, thank you."

As soon as he moved on another man approached her. He'd been only a few feet away and she'd seen him a few times during the evening. The tall stranger with tanned skin and black hair was hard to miss, especially when she'd caught him eyeing her more than once. He'd been smiling her way for a while, and now he was closing the gap between them.

"You turned down champagne and you're not dancing," he said in lieu of hello. "One would think you're not having a good time."

Kate smiled, trying to place his accent. Not Greek. Mikos had friends and acquaintances all over the world, so who knew where he was from?

"I'm having a great time," she told him. "It's so beautiful, I'm just taking in all the scenery."

"I've been taking in the scenery, too."

His eyes held hers, and the implication was not lost on her. At one time that line may have worked on her, but she felt absolutely no tingling or giddiness in her stomach when this man approached, blatantly hitting on her. Good thing, because she was certain she didn't have the strength to be tied up with more than one man.

"Would you care to dance?"

Kate glanced around. She hadn't seen Luc for a while, and more than likely he was schmoozing with people he rarely got to see. Besides, it wasn't as if he had a claim on her. He'd pretty much brought her here for one of two reasons: as a lame plan B or to keep an eye on her. Either way, he'd ignored her most of the evening, and she was entitled to some fun, too.

"I'd love to."

Kate slid her hand through the stranger's arm and held on to the crook of his elbow as he led her to the dance floor. When he found an opening, he spun her around until she was in his arms. Kate purposely kept her body from lining up against his as she placed her hand on his shoulder and curled her fingers around his outstretched hand.

"I'm Kate, by the way."

A smile kicked up at the corner of his mouth. "I'm Lars."

"Pleasure to meet you," she said as he turned her in a wide circle. "You're a great dancer."

"I'm actually a professional ballroom dancer." He laughed as he led her into a slower dance when the song changed. "Stick with me tonight and we'll be the envy of all the other couples."

Kate couldn't help but laugh at his blatant ego. "I should tell you, I'm taken."

Well, she wasn't exactly taken, but she was having another man's child, and she was in love with said man, even though he didn't return the feelings. So she felt it necessary to let Lars know he stood no chance with her.

He leaned in closer to whisper into her ear. "Yet he's not here and I am." When he leaned back, his smile remained in place. "Don't worry. I just wanted to dance with the most stunning woman in the room."

"I think that honor goes to the bride," Kate corrected.

Darcy had looked magnificent in a fitted ivory dress with an elegant lace overlay, complete with a lace train that would make any princess envious. Darcy had looked like a character from a fairy-tale romance, and her Prince Charming at the end of the aisle had had nothing but love on his face for his bride.

Would Kate ever find that? Would she ever find a man who looked at her as though there was nothing greater in the world than the fact she lived in it?

"Uh-oh. I'm going to start questioning my skills if you keep frowning."

Kate shook the thoughts away. "Your dance skills

are perfect, though I'm sure you already knew that. I think the jet lag is getting to me."

Not to mention the pregnancy…which she and Luc still hadn't discussed announcing. So for now, she was keeping it to herself. Granted, not many people knew who she was, but the same could not be said for Luc.

Lars opened his mouth to say something, but his eyes darted over Kate's shoulder as he came to a stop.

"It's time to go, Kate."

Turning, she saw Luc standing less than a foot away.

"I'm dancing right now," she commented, not letting go of her partner's hand. "I can find my way back. You go on."

Luc pasted on a deadly smile and glanced at Lars. "I'm sure he will understand. Won't you, Lars?"

The other man merely nodded and stepped back, but not before kissing Kate's hand. "It was truly my pleasure."

Then he disappeared in the crowd of dancers, most likely heading to find another partner. Kate jerked around, clenching her teeth.

"Watch what you say," Luc warned as he took her arm and led her away. "I've got plenty to tell you, too, so save it until we're alone."

"What makes you think I'm going anywhere with you?" she said through gritted teeth. "You can't tell me who to spend time with."

Luc's fingers tightened around her arm as he leaned in closer to her side. "Oh, we're going to be alone, and I'm going to explain to you exactly why that little scene will never happen again."

Fifteen

Luc was seething. He hated like hell that his emotions had overridden common sense, but the second he'd seen Kate dancing with Lars, all rational thoughts had vanished.

The palace was big enough to house the special guests of the bride and groom, so Luc was glad he didn't have to drag Kate too far before he lit into her.

He'd purposely avoided her as much as he could because of her body-hugging dress. That damn gown nearly had him babbling like some horny teen, but he'd somehow managed to keep his tongue in his mouth when he first saw her. Luc knew if he'd stayed too close to Kate this evening, there would be no way to hide his obvious attraction.

And he couldn't let the attraction show, because Kate might try to use that...for what? Wasn't he set on using her?

Only now that he'd seen her in the arms of another man, the game had just changed. Luc wanted her. Right now.

He reached the second floor and headed down the hall to his suite. He had no clue if Kate was deliberately toying with him, but she had him tied in knots he'd never be able to untangle thanks to that little stunt with Lars…a man Luc despised.

"I want to go to my room," she demanded, yanking from his hold as soon as he stopped in front of a set of double doors. "I'm not going in there with you."

Resting his hand on the knob, Luc threw a smirk over his shoulder. "You are."

Kate's eyes narrowed. "No, my room is down the hall."

Before he realized his intentions, he'd pulled her around, wedging her body between his and the door. "Your room is right here until I'm done with you."

"Well, I'm already done talking. You were completely rude down there. You can't just—"

His mouth covered hers. If she was done talking, then he'd find better use for that mouth and ignore all the damn red flags waving around in his mind. He didn't care about all the reasons this was wrong, didn't care that moments ago she'd been in another man's arms. Right now she was in *his* arms, and he was taking full advantage of that lush, curvy body.

Kate's hands came up to his shoulders to push at him, but Luc settled his palms on her hips and pressed against her. Suddenly, her fingertips were curling into his tuxedo jacket.

The feel of her rounded hips beneath her killer dress was just as potent as this steamy kiss. Kate tipped her head slightly, but the silent invitation was all he needed to trace a path with his tongue down the column of her throat.

"Luc," she panted in a whisper. "We're in the hallway."

Gripping her hips, Luc rested his forehead against her collarbone. "You make me crazy, Kate. Out of my mind crazy."

Reaching around her, he opened the door. As soon as they were inside, he closed it, flicked the lock and leaned back against it.

"Did you bring me to your suite to talk or to have sex?" she asked, her arms folded across her beautifully displayed chest. "Because I know what you said, but that episode in the hall has me confused."

Luc remained where he was as he raked a hand down his face. "Lars isn't a good idea." He ignored her narrowed gaze. "Seeing you in his arms... He's a player, Kate."

She held Luc's eyes for a moment before she burst out laughing. "You're kidding me. You interrupt my dance, you manhandle me out of the ballroom and up the steps, and then you attempt to make out with me in the hallway because you're jealous? And you're calling someone else a player?"

"First of all, I'm not jealous." Wow, that almost sounded convincing. "Second, I never manhandled you, and third, you were completely on board with what was going on in the hallway. You moaned."

Kate rolled her eyes and turned to stalk across the open suite. "I did not moan."

Luc didn't know which view was better, the front of Kate's gown with the glimpse of her breasts or the back, where he could fully focus on the perfection of her shape. She stood at the desk, her hands resting on it, her head dropped forward.

"I don't know what you want from me." Her voice was so low he had to move closer to hear. "I won't allow you to pull me all these directions because of your out-of-control emotions, Luc. You know how strongly I feel for you, and yet you continue to torture me."

He was counting on those feelings to get him what he wanted. As much as he hated to admit it, he needed Kate in every way.

Before Luc realized it, he'd completely closed the distance between them. Sliding his hands around her waist, he pressed his palms against her still-flat stomach and jerked her body against his.

"You think you don't torture me?" he asked, his lips brushing the side of her ear. She shivered against him. "You think seeing you dressed like this, moving your body against another man's, isn't pure hell?"

"Why do you care?"

"Because just the thought of you turns me inside out. Because knowing how sexy you are wearing only a smile that I put on your lips turns me on faster than anything."

Luc eased her around and framed her face with his hands. "Because I'm so torn up over what to do about you, all I can think of is getting you out of this damn dress and seeing if this chemistry is real or if it only existed when I thought we were engaged."

Kate's breath caught in her throat as she stared back at him. "I can't sleep with you as an experiment, Luc. I love you." Her voice cracked and her eyes filled with tears. "I'm not hiding how I feel. I can't. But I also can't be used on a whim, whenever you get an itch you need to scratch."

"You're more than an itch."

"What am I?" she whispered.

Luc couldn't put a label to this madness that had become his life. He'd planned on seduction, but he hadn't planned on the jealousy that had speared through him moments ago. Kate was his.

"You're the woman I'm about to put on this desk and strip until she's wearing nothing but that pendant. You're the woman who is going to forget everything else but what's happening right here, right now."

"Sex won't solve anything."

"No, but it will take the edge off for both of us."

Luc leaned closer, rubbing his lips across hers, so slowly. He reached around, found the zipper and eased it down. When the material parted in the back, he splayed his hand across her bare skin, relishing the way she trembled against him.

"Tell me you don't want this," he murmured against her mouth. "Tell me you don't want to see what happens right now between us, and you can walk out that door before we get too far to turn back."

Luc started to peel her dress away from her body. He stepped back just enough for the gown to ease down and puddle at her feet, leaving her standing in a strapless bra and matching panties, and that purple stone that rested against her flawless skin. Trailing his fingertips over the swell of her breasts, Luc smiled when she arched against his touch.

"Say the word, Kate, and I'll stop."

Her eyes closed as she dipped her head back. "You don't play fair."

"Oh, baby, I haven't even begun to play."

She was going to put a stop to this...then Luc had to go and say those words dripping in seduction while he tempted her with just the tips of his fingers. The man was potent. He knew exactly what to do to get her aroused, to get her wanting more.

Why was she letting this happen? He had no intention of professing his love. He wouldn't even give her a straight answer earlier when she'd asked who she was to him.

Yet here she stood, in her heels, her underwear and goose bumps from his touch.

How could she deny him? How could she deny herself? All she wanted was this man, and here he was. If she had even a glimmer of a chance to get him to see how good they were together, she'd take it. Her heart couldn't break any more…could it?

Luc's mouth followed the trail of his fingertips along the tops of her breasts, just over the lacy bra cups. "I'll take your silence as a go-ahead."

Kate slid her fingers into his inky-black hair as she looked down at him. "I can't say no to you."

"I didn't intend to let you."

He crushed her body to his as his mouth claimed hers. Kate shoved his tux jacket off and to the floor. Without breaking contact, she started unbuttoning his shirt. The need to feel his skin next to hers was all-consuming.

Luc wrapped his hands around her waist and lifted her onto the desk. He jerked his shirt off, sending the rest of the buttons popping and scattering across the hardwood floor. The sight of that bare chest, the familiar tattoo and a smattering of chest hair had her heart beating in double time and her body aching.

He stepped between her thighs, encircled her torso with his arms and jerked her to the edge.

"Wrap your legs around me."

His husky demand had her obeying in an instant.

What was it about this man that could have her throwing all common sense aside and practically bowing to his every wish?

Love. That's all it boiled down to. If she didn't love him, if she hadn't been in love with him for some time, she never would've allowed herself to be put in this vulnerable position.

Luc managed to work off her bra and panties with a quick, clever snap and torn material. The fact he was so eager sent warmth spreading through her. She'd made him this reckless, this out of control.

And that right there told her she had the upper hand.

Squeezing her legs tighter against his narrow hips, Kate gripped his head and pulled him down to her mouth. Instantly, he opened, groaning against her. His hands seemed to be everywhere at once. How else could she explain all the shivers, the rippling, the tingling?

"Lean back," he muttered against her lips.

Kate leaned back on the smooth desk, resting her weight on her elbows. When his eyes locked onto hers, the moment he joined them, Kate couldn't help the burn in her throat, the instant tears pricking her eyes. Even though their bond may have started off with a lie, it didn't diminish the fact she loved him. He cared for her more than he let on, too, or they wouldn't be here right now.

Kate shoved aside all worry, all thoughts, and reveled in the moment. Luc was here, with her. He was making love to her in a slow, passionate way that was polar opposite to the frantic way he'd stripped them both moments ago. Did she dare hope he wanted more from her?

Luc leaned over her, kissed her softly and rested his forehead against hers. With Luc's hands gripping her waist, she held on to his shoulders and kept her gaze on him.

Within moments, her body climbed, tightened. Luc muttered something she didn't quite understand. Between the Portuguese and the low whisper, his words were lost. But then his own body stiffened against hers as he squeezed his eyes shut.

Once the tremors ceased, Luc picked her up and carried her to his bed, draped in gold-and-white sheers. He laid her down and slid in beside her, pulling her body against his.

"Sleep." His hands immediately went to her stomach. "Rest for our baby."

Kate closed her eyes, wondering if this blossom of hope in her chest would still be there come morning. Wondering if the man she'd fallen in love with was actually starting to love her back.

Sixteen

Nausea hit her hard. Kate prayed that if she just lay still the queasiness would pass. Until now, she'd had no symptoms of pregnancy, save for the missed period and being tired. Those things she could handle.

As for the man who had put her in this situation in the first place, well, that was another story.

Kate tried to focus on the fact she'd spent the night in Luc's bed, this time with him fully aware of who she was and why she was there. Surely that meant something. Surely they'd crossed some major barrier and things would only get better from here.

Kate wasn't naive, but she was hopeful. She had to be.

But the bed next to her was empty, cool. She sat up, clutching the sheet to her chest. That abrupt movement had her stomach roiling. Bad idea. She closed her eyes and waited for the dizziness to pass before she risked scanning the oversize bedroom for Luc.

He stood near the floor-to-ceiling window, sipping a cup of coffee. His bare back, with bronze skin and dark ink, stared back at her. She didn't want this to be awkward, but she had no idea what to say, how to act. She'd selfishly given in to her desires last night, not thinking of consequences. Well, she had thought of them, but she'd chosen to weigh heavily on the side of optimism.

Her legs shifted beneath the warm satin sheets. Luc glanced over his shoulder at the sound, then focused his attention back on the sunrise. She had to admit the orange sky glowing with radiant beauty was a sight to behold, but was he not going to say anything?

Please, please don't let this be awkward.

Kate eased back against the headboard and tucked the sheet beneath her arms to stay fully covered. Not that he hadn't seen all of her multiple times, but she was getting a vibe that this wasn't going to be a good morning, and the last thing she wanted to do was go into battle fully naked.

"I've been trying to figure out what the hell to do here."

His words sliced right through the beauty of the morning, killing any hope she'd built. His tone wasn't promising. If anything, it was angry, confused.

"I watched you sleep," he went on, still not looking at her. Damn it, why wouldn't he turn around? "I even tried to rest, but there are so many thoughts going around in my mind that I don't even know where to start or what's real."

"Everything that happened in this room last night was real." If nothing else, she wanted, needed, him to realize that. "Did you only bring me here for sex, Luc?"

Speaking her fear aloud had her heart cracking. She

wanted to be strong, she truly did, but there was only so much a woman could take.

"I wanted you." Luc turned to face her, but made no move to cross the room. "I've fought this urge since you came to work for me. I got engaged to another woman knowing full well I wanted you physically. Even after that engagement ended, I still had this ache for you, even though I knew I couldn't act on it."

Kate clutched the sheet as he went on.

"I wasn't in a good spot when we were at the beach house," he continued. "I was an emotional wreck, and I never should've had you come with me, not when I knew just how much I wanted you."

Her eyes darted back to his. "You were angry with me," she reminded him. "Before the accident, you kissed me—"

"I kissed you because I couldn't keep fighting the attraction. I kissed you out of anger toward myself, and then I was even angrier. I was rough with you, so I stomped off like a child."

And then he'd been injured and forgotten everything.

Kate licked her dry lips. "I don't know what to say."

"Honestly, I don't, either." Luc slowly walked toward the bed, coming to stand at the end of it and holding her gaze. "There's part of me that wants to be able to trust you again, but you hurt me, Kate. I never thought that was possible. And that's what had me up all night."

Kate cringed at his harsh words. What could she say? He was right.

"I thought we were going to move past that," she stated, praying the possibility even existed. "You said we'd move on, that we'd have a professional relationship."

Luc's arms stretched wide as he eyed the bed. "Is

this professional? I sure as hell don't feel like your boss right now, Kate. You're having my child, the next heir to the throne after me."

"And is that all I am, then? The mother to the next heir?" She needed more. Even after her lies, she deserved to know. "Are you using my feelings against me? You know how I feel, and you got so jealous last night. Was that all to stroke your ego or to puff your chest out because you're in control?"

Luc propped his hands on his narrow hips as he stared down at her. He'd put on his black tuxedo pants, but hadn't buttoned them. It was hard to sit here and discuss all of this with him half-dressed and her wearing a sheet, but Kate had her pride, and she refused to give in to her body's needs. She didn't need Luc; she wanted him. Yes, it hurt to know he didn't feel the same, but she wasn't going to beg…ever.

His silence was deafening. Kate shook her hair away from her face. The nausea hadn't lessened; if anything, she felt worse. She placed a hand beside her hip on the bed, closed her eyes and took a deep breath.

"Kate?"

The mattress dipped beside her. When Luc grabbed her hand, she pulled back. "No." She met his worried gaze. "I'm not playing the pregnancy card for your sympathy and attention. You don't get to pick and choose when it's convenient to show affection."

"You're pale. Are you all right?"

If only he would have cared first thing this morning instead of starting this day with voicing his doubts and crushing her hopes.

"I'm dizzy. It's to be expected." She shifted, scooting a bit farther away from him. "I'm not going to be pulled in different directions depending on your moods, either. You either want me, on a personal level and not just for sex, or you don't. If my dancing with some guy bothers you, then maybe you need to reevaluate your feelings. But don't come to me again unless you're sure I'm more than just a warm body to you."

Slowly, Luc came to his feet and nodded. "I plan on having you, Kate. I plan on marrying you, actually. You'll become my wife before my birthday. I'll secure the title and you'll get to live out whatever fantasy you had when you wanted to play the engaged couple."

"What?" Shock replaced her nausea instantly. "I'm not marrying you just so you can get a title. I want to marry for love."

Luc's eyes narrowed. "You say you love me, so why not marry me?"

"Because you don't love me. I won't be used as a pawn in your royal quest."

Air whooshed from her lungs. She'd never thought herself naive, but that's exactly what she was. She should've gone into this with eyes wide-open and seen his motivations for what they were...lust and greed. Any love between them was absolutely one-sided, and she had no one to blame but herself...yet again.

She should've seen this coming, should've known nothing would ever get in the way of the great Luc Silva and his crown. The man she'd grown to love from the island was just as fake as their engagement. Then, he'd been warm, open. Now he was all business.

"I'm going back to the palace as soon as I get my stuff together," she told him. "I'll have the pilot come back whenever you want to leave, but I won't be flying with you. I also won't be working for you. I'll finish out my duties for the next couple of weeks, but after that, I'm done."

"As my wife, I wouldn't expect you to work for me."

Kate clenched her teeth, praying she didn't burst into angry tears. "I won't be your wife."

Luc shoved his hands in his pockets, hesitated, then made his way to the door. "Don't make any hasty decisions. I'll leave you to get your dress back on."

Then he was gone, leaving only the deafening sound of the door clicking shut as she sat there in the rumpled sheets.

That was it? Luc may have walked out of this conversation, but he wasn't going to back down on this ridiculous notion of them getting married. Kate needed to prepare herself, because this fight was just getting started.

She tossed back the sheet and was thankful she wasn't dizzy when she got to her feet. At least she had one thing going for her this morning.

Of course, now she had to put on her dress from last night and do the walk of shame down the wide, long hallway to her own suite, to change and pack. Which was fine, because she wasn't staying any longer. If he planned on using her, using her feelings against her in some ploy to get ahead, then maybe he wasn't the man she loved at all. Maybe she'd been living a lie this entire time…

There was no way she could continue working for Luc indefinitely. No way she could look at him every single day and know she was good enough for sex, but not good enough to build a life with if the throne wasn't at stake. They'd made a baby and he still was only looking out for his title. Well, she sure as hell wasn't sticking around to see him parade his possible future wives in and out of his life.

Kate had been a fool to think their intimacy had

changed Luc's mind. The struggle of seeing him every day, knowing he didn't return her love, would be just too hurtful.

When she returned to the palace, she would call her parents and make plans. She would finish up the projects she and Luc had begun, and then she needed to get away. She needed to focus on what was truly important in her life.

Luc brought the sledgehammer up and swung it through the partial non-load-bearing wall. Busting this drywall to expand the living space with the kitchen wasn't even remotely helping to quell his frustration and anger. All he was doing was working up a good sweat and a bit of nostalgia from when he and Kate had torn into the bathroom.

When Luc had gotten back to the palace, he'd taken his boat—sans guards, much to Kate's father's disapproval— and headed to his beach house. Luc knew the workers would be done for the day, and since the house was only an hour from the palace, he needed time to think, to reflect on what an insufferable jerk he'd been in that bedroom three days ago.

His intention had been to get Kate to agree to marry him. He hadn't cared about her feelings. But the way she'd sat there, all rumpled in a mess of satin sheets, as she'd stared up at him with hurt in her eyes, had seriously gotten to him. He hadn't expected to feel anything beyond want and need for her. Yet it was hard to ignore the constant lump of guilt that kept creeping up when he thought of how he'd broken her so fast, with so few words.

Luc eased the sledgehammer down on the rubble and wiped his arm across his forehead. His mother would probably die if she saw he had blisters on his hands from manual labor, but he needed the outlet. Unfortunately, it wasn't doing the job.

And it didn't help that Kate was everywhere in this house. The empty yellow vase on the scarred dining table mocked him. He couldn't even look at the damn shower in his master suite. The balcony, the chaise in the living room, the bed, the beach… The memories flooded his mind. She'd touched literally every surface here.

Just as she'd touched every part of him.

Luc reached behind his neck and yanked his T-shirt over his head. His cell vibrated in his pocket and he thought about ignoring it, but with Kate being pregnant, he had to be on full alert.

Pulling the cell out, he glanced at the screen. Swallowing a curse, he let out a sigh and answered.

"Yes?"

"You rushed out of here and didn't take a guard?"

His mother's question didn't require an answer, because she already knew. "I needed to be alone."

"That's not smart. You can't be taking off like this, Lucas. You know your birthday is less than two months away. You need to be home so we can figure out what we're going to do."

Luc raked a hand over his damp face and stared out at the sun, which was starting to dip toward the horizon.

"I just needed a few days to myself."

"Is this about Kate? Darling, I know she hurt you, but that poor girl is miserable. I didn't want to say anything, but since the wedding she's been looking pale and drained."

Luc straightened. "Is she sick?"

"I'd guess she's pregnant."

Silence filled the line and Luc's heart sank. They hadn't said a word to anybody, and the pain in his mother's tone came through loud and clear.

"We haven't told anyone," Luc stated in a low voice, suddenly feeling like a kid again for lying to his mother. "She just found out before the wedding, and we had a bit of a fight. Is she okay?"

"A fight?" Of course his mom honed in on that and not his question. "Lucas, the woman is carrying your child and you argue with her? No wonder she looks exhausted. She's been working like a dog since she got back. That's why I wanted to know why you left the palace so suddenly."

Luc gripped the phone. "It's best if I'm not there right now."

"I think you two need to talk. If you're worried about the no-fraternizing rule, I think we can make an exception for Kate. Maybe she's the answer to—"

"I've already thought of that," he interrupted, cutting her off. "Kate doesn't want to marry me."

"Why don't you come home," his mother stated. "We can't solve any problems with you brooding alone."

He glanced at the mess he'd made. It wasn't as if he knew what to do next, but the contractors had done an amazing job of renovating the bathroom he and Kate had torn into. They'd come to finish the kitchen once Luc gave the go-ahead after this wall was gone.

"I'm leaving now," he told his mother. "Tell Kate I want to see her."

"I'll see what I can do, but she may have left for the day."

If she'd left, he'd go to her place. She didn't live too far from the palace, and if he had any say, she'd be inside that palace by the time their baby came.

Anything else was unacceptable.

Having her that last time had changed something in him, and nearly changed his marriage plan. That's why he'd been up all night, second-guessing his motives. He'd thought he could check out emotionally, but he felt too much—guilt, desire…more.

He'd hurt her in ways he'd never, ever imagined he could. Yet she still did her job. She'd still come with him to the wedding. She still supported him.

And he loved her. His feelings were as simple and as complicated as that. He loved Kate with everything he had and he'd messed up—man, had he messed up.

Luc needed to tell her how he felt. More important, he needed to show her. Saying the words was easy; proving to Kate how much she meant to him would be the hurdle. But he hadn't gone through all of this to give up now. Kate was his and he damn well wasn't going to let her go.

Seventeen

It had been nearly a week since he'd last talked to Kate, and he was going out of his mind.

He'd come back to his office and found a letter of resignation on his desk. She'd left a message through her mother that she was fine and the baby was fine, but she wanted to be on her own for a bit.

A bit was longer than he could stand.

He'd lived without this woman for too long and refused to live that way another second.

His birthday was fast approaching, but even the looming date hadn't entered his mind. For the past few days all that had played over and over was how stupid he'd been, how heartless and crass he'd been with his words, his actions. No wonder Kate wanted to leave, to steer clear of him. She loved him and he'd proposed to her with the pretense that he was doing so only to climb higher on the royal ladder.

He hadn't needed much time after their last night together to realize walking away had been a mistake. Letting her believe he wanted her only for the crown was wrong.

Luc wanted Kate because she made him whole.

It had taken him some time to get the information on her whereabouts from her parents, and to have the construction crew finish some of the renovations on his beach home. He'd pulled some strings to get her here, but he wanted this to be perfect when he finally revealed the house and his true feelings. Nothing but the best for Kate from here on out.

He'd taken that extra time to find out more about the woman he loved. And he hoped the surprise he'd planned would help her understand just how much he wanted her in his life.

Luc stood in the living room watching the water, waiting for that familiar boat to dock. He'd recruited the help of Kate's parents. Of course, in order to do that, he'd had to pull out all the stops and really grovel to them. If everything worked out the way he'd hoped, every ego-bursting, pride-crushing moment would be worth it.

When the boat finally came into view, Luc's nerves really kicked into gear. He might have planned every bit of this evening, but Kate ultimately held all the power and control.

Her father helped her up onto the dock, leaned forward for a hug and watched as Kate mounted the steps. Luc moved to the doorway and waved as the man began to pull the boat away from the berth.

By the time Kate got to the top of the steps, Luc's heart was beating faster than ever. She lifted her head, pushing her windblown hair away from her face. The second her eyes locked onto his, Luc felt that familiar punch to his gut. The punch that said if she turned him down he would be absolutely crushed and broken.

"I was hoping you wouldn't put up a fight," he told her, remaining in the doorway.

"I was tempted to jump overboard a couple of times, but I knew my dad would only go in after me." She clasped her hands together and remained still. "What am I doing here, Luc, and why am I being held hostage?"

"You're not a hostage," he countered.

She glanced over her shoulder before looking back. "My father left with the boat and the only other one here is yours. By my accounts, I'm here with no way out except with your permission."

"Come inside."

Her brow quirked as she crossed her arms over her chest…a chest that was more voluptuous than when he'd seen her last.

"Please," he added, when she didn't move. "Please come inside so we can talk."

Finally, she moved forward, and Luc let her pass him and enter first. The familiar, floral scent teased his senses and mocked him. He'd lain awake at night imagining that scent, pretending she was by his side.

"Oh, Luc."

Her gasp was enough to have him smiling. "Looks a little different, doesn't it?"

He watched her survey the newly designed, open floor plan. Thick columns stood as support beams, but they didn't take away from the romantic ambience, they merely added to it. He'd left the back wall of patio doors open, to put the Mediterranean on full display.

"It's gorgeous," she exclaimed, running her hand along the marble-topped table behind the sofa. "This was all done so fast."

"I wanted it done before I invited you back." He remained in the doorway, but kept his eyes on her as she walked through the living area and kitchen. "I even helped the contractors and learned how to do more than tear things down."

She stopped by the old dining table and her eyes landed on the yellow vase, then darted across the room to him.

"I couldn't get rid of either of those," he told her. "We shared too many meals at that table, and even though it's not new, it reminds me of you. Every time I see that vase I think of how excited you were that day at the market."

She picked up the vase, running her hands around it. For a moment Luc worried she might launch it at his head, but she finally set it down and turned back to face him. With her arms crossed over her midsection, she let out a sigh.

"What do you want, Luc?"

Her eyes held his. Now that they were face-to-face, he couldn't deny the force that hovered between them.

"Are you feeling okay?" he asked, taking slow, cautious steps toward her. "Everything all right with our baby?"

"We're both doing great," she informed him. "And you could've texted or called or replied to the emails I sent."

"You sent final work emails through your father."

She nodded. "That's because I quit, remember? I've outlined your next year of engagements. I'm assuming you came up with a way to secure your title? Is that why you can bother with me now?"

"No. I didn't secure the title."

Kate gasped. "Your birthday is only weeks away."

"I'm aware of that." He stood directly in front of her, so close she had to tip her head up to look him in the eyes. "That's why you're here."

Her lips thinned as she narrowed her gaze at him. "You've got to be kidding me. You brought me here to use me? You still think I'm going to swoon, fall at your feet and marry you so you can get a shiny new crown?"

Just as she started to push past him, Luc grabbed her arm and halted her escape. "No. I think you're going to listen to me and look in my eyes when I tell you how much I love you."

Those dark eyes held his, but he saw no emotion there. "Did you hear me?"

"I hear you just fine," she said through clenched teeth. "How convenient that you love me right before you're set to lose it all if you don't have a wife."

He turned to face her fully as he gripped both her bare shoulders. "You and these damn sexy strapless dresses," he muttered, stroking her skin with his thumbs. "Cause me to forget the powerful speech I was about to make. I'm pretty proud, considering it's the first one I've had to write for myself."

"I don't want to hear your speech and I don't want you touching me."

Luc smiled. "Then why is the pulse at the base of your neck pounding as fast as my heart? You may lie to yourself, Kate, but your body is telling me the truth."

Her eyes widened. "Oh, no. You brought me here for sex? You think I'll fall back into bed with you and then, in the throes of passion, agree to a marriage?"

Luc laughed, then kissed her full on the mouth before easing back. "Your imagination is running away with you and I'm royally screwing this up."

"That's the only thing that's getting screwed tonight."

His heart was so full, he couldn't help but keep smiling. "I've missed that smart mouth."

Kate didn't say a word, didn't move and didn't make any attempt to touch him.

"Tell me I didn't mess things up so badly that I've lost you forever."

"You never fully had me," she told him. "I wanted everything with you, but went about it the wrong way. Then you decided to use my love and try to force me into marriage. That's no foundation to build a relationship on."

"We both messed up," he agreed. "I never meant to hurt you, but I was so confused. I wanted to trust my feelings, but how could I when I couldn't even trust you? I thought if you wanted me so badly, you'd marry me and I'd get the title. I didn't realize you truly had no ulterior motive."

"I understand why you couldn't trust me." She reached up, wrapped her hands around his wrists and pulled his hands off her shoulders. "What I can't understand is why you used my feelings against me, why you made love to me at Mikos's wedding and then acted like you had no clue where to slot me in your life."

Luc shoved his hands in his pockets. She didn't want to be touched, and right now he was dying to have her in his arms. This was going to be trickier than he'd thought, but he wasn't giving up. She'd come, she was talking to him and that had to mean a lot.

"I have something to show you."

He walked to the desk tucked in the corner of the room and grabbed the email he'd printed out. When he handed it to her, she didn't take it.

"Please?"

Kate slid the paper from his grasp. Luc watched her face as she read. When her eyes filled with tears, her hand came up to cover her quivering chin and her lips, Luc knew she wasn't completely lost to him.

She clutched the letter to her chest. "You went to the orphanage?"

"I did." And he'd loved every minute of it. "I met Carly and Thomas. I was told they were friends of yours."

Kate nodded, the jerky movement causing a tear to spill. "I love those two so much. They are such sweet kids, but most people want to adopt new babies. The twins are nine, but they have such big hearts and they say they want the babies to go to new homes. Still, I know they long for a set of parents to love them."

"I was told it's hard, too, because most people are only looking to adopt one," he added.

"I try to get there to visit them as often as I can," she said, swiping at her eyes. "I call them if I get too busy working and can't make it."

"They're at the orphanage you were living in as a baby." Luc cupped her damp face. "And that's why they are so important to you. I can completely see why you wanted me to go visit. Those little kids thought talking to a real prince was so neat. I didn't talk much about the royalty side of my life with Carly and Thomas, but we did discuss Portuguese culture, and they were so fascinated."

"I can't believe you went and didn't tell me," she exclaimed.

"Actually, we just missed each other. When I arrived, I was told you had left the day before."

Kate's eyes widened. "I wish I'd known."

"Why, Kate? Would you have stayed there? Would you have waited for me?"

She shook her head. "I—I don't know."

"I want to start over with you." That sounded so

lame he laughed. "I've been miserable without you and I went to that orphanage not because you kept asking me to, but because I wanted to know more about you. I wanted to know more about the woman I had fallen in love with. I love you, Kate. I want a life with you, a life just like the one we had when we were all alone here."

Kate closed her eyes as her body fell into his. Her forehead rested against his chest. "You don't mean all of that," she whispered. "Because if you even think I can just try this out, or be with you because of some tradition, you're wrong."

When she lifted her head, Luc smoothed her hair away from her damp cheeks. "I don't want to try it, Kate. I want to do it. My calling you here has nothing to do with the throne, my birthday or the baby. I mean, I want to build a family with you, but I'm not using the baby to do so. I want you for you. The days we spent here were some of the best of my life. I want more days like that, and nobody else will do. You're it for me, Kate."

When her mouth parted in another gasp, he kissed her. Luc nipped at her lips and nearly cried when she responded and opened for him.

The gentle, tender kiss had that sliver of hope in his chest practically exploding now.

"I missed you," he murmured against her lips. "I missed holding you, I missed watching you cook, I missed seeing you smile, and even arguing with you over stupid things like my schedule. I missed seeing you wearing my ring."

Her brows drew in as Luc pulled the amethyst ring from his pocket.

"Você vai casar comigo?" he asked.

Will you marry me?

"Not because of the throne, not because of anything else but us," he quickly said, before she got the wrong idea of his intentions. "I can feel utter fullness and love only with you, Kate. You're the only one who can make me complete."

Without waiting for her reply, he slid the ring onto her finger and gripped her hand in his. "This is where the ring belongs, until I can get you a diamond or whatever you want."

Kate stared down at her hand and said nothing. She studied the ring, even toyed with it before she smiled up at him. "I don't want another ring. I want this one. It's exactly what I would have chosen, and I don't need anything more."

"Does this mean you'll marry me?" he asked.

Kate threw her arms around his neck, buried her face against his skin and squeezed him tight. "I'll marry you, Luc. I'll raise babies with you and grow old with you."

Luc crushed her body to his and let out the first good breath he'd had since she stepped into his house. No, their house.

Kate jerked back. "Wait. We need to marry soon. Your birthday—"

"It will be fine. My father may have rigged the law a tad to buy us a few extra weeks. I want to give you the wedding you deserve."

"I don't want a huge, highly publicized wedding. Is that okay?"

Luc framed her face, sliding his thumb across her full bottom lip. "Perfectly fine with me. But right now I'd rather have you in my shower, where I can properly show you how much I've missed you."

"I do love that shower of yours."

He kissed her smile. "After I make love to you, we

can discuss the wedding. Oh, and the fact I'd like to adopt Carly and Thomas. I wanted to talk to you first. With the new baby and all I wasn't sure—"

Kate's mouth cut him off as she rained kisses all over his lips, his chin, his cheeks. "Yes, yes, yes. I'd love to have them with me. I love those two so much. I just felt such a connection the first time I saw them."

"I did, too, honey." Luc picked her up and headed toward the master suite. "We'll discuss that later, too."

"You can't carry me," she cried. "I've gained weight."

His eyes dipped to her chest. "I've noticed, and I'm certainly not complaining."

She slapped his shoulder. "That's so typical of a man, to say that when bigger boobs are involved."

"There better never be another man eyeing your boobs," he scolded. "That's my job."

Kate's head fell against his shoulder as she laced her fingers together behind his neck. "Always, Luc. You're the only man for me."

* * * * *

*If you loved this royal hero from
Jules Bennett
pick up her other royal novels*

*BEHIND PALACE DOORS
WHAT THE PRINCE WANTS*

MILLS & BOON®
Hardback – July 2015

ROMANCE

The Ruthless Greek's Return	Sharon Kendrick
Bound by the Billionaire's Baby	Cathy Williams
Married for Amari's Heir	Maisey Yates
A Taste of Sin	Maggie Cox
Sicilian's Shock Proposal	Carol Marinelli
Vows Made in Secret	Louise Fuller
The Sheikh's Wedding Contract	Andie Brock
Tycoon's Delicious Debt	Susanna Carr
A Bride for the Italian Boss	Susan Meier
The Millionaire's True Worth	Rebecca Winters
The Earl's Convenient Wife	Marion Lennox
Vettori's Damsel in Distress	Liz Fielding
Unlocking Her Surgeon's Heart	Fiona Lowe
Her Playboy's Secret	Tina Beckett
The Doctor She Left Behind	Scarlet Wilson
Taming Her Navy Doc	Amy Ruttan
A Promise...to a Proposal?	Kate Hardy
Her Family for Keeps	Molly Evans
Seduced by the Spare Heir	Andrea Laurence
A Royal Amnesia Scandal	Jules Bennett

MILLS & BOON®
Large Print – July 2015

ROMANCE

The Taming of Xander Sterne	Carole Mortimer
In the Brazilian's Debt	Susan Stephens
At the Count's Bidding	Caitlin Crews
The Sheikh's Sinful Seduction	Dani Collins
The Real Romero	Cathy Williams
His Defiant Desert Queen	Jane Porter
Prince Nadir's Secret Heir	Michelle Conder
The Renegade Billionaire	Rebecca Winters
The Playboy of Rome	Jennifer Faye
Reunited with Her Italian Ex	Lucy Gordon
Her Knight in the Outback	Nikki Logan

HISTORICAL

The Soldier's Dark Secret	Marguerite Kaye
Reunited with the Major	Anne Herries
The Rake to Rescue Her	Julia Justiss
Lord Gawain's Forbidden Mistress	Carol Townend
A Debt Paid in Marriage	Georgie Lee

MEDICAL

How to Find a Man in Five Dates	Tina Beckett
Breaking Her No-Dating Rule	Amalie Berlin
It Happened One Night Shift	Amy Andrews
Tamed by Her Army Doc's Touch	Lucy Ryder
A Child to Bind Them	Lucy Clark
The Baby That Changed Her Life	Louisa Heaton

MILLS & BOON®
Hardback – August 2015

ROMANCE

The Greek Demands His Heir	Lynne Graham
The Sinner's Marriage Redemption	Annie West
His Sicilian Cinderella	Carol Marinelli
Captivated by the Greek	Julia James
The Perfect Cazorla Wife	Michelle Smart
Claimed for His Duty	Tara Pammi
The Marakaios Baby	Kate Hewitt
Billionaire's Ultimate Acquisition	Melanie Milburne
Return of the Italian Tycoon	Jennifer Faye
His Unforgettable Fiancée	Teresa Carpenter
Hired by the Brooding Billionaire	Kandy Shepherd
A Will, a Wish...a Proposal	Jessica Gilmore
Hot Doc from Her Past	Tina Beckett
Surgeons, Rivals...Lovers	Amalie Berlin
Best Friend to Perfect Bride	Jennifer Taylor
Resisting Her Rebel Doc	Joanna Neil
A Baby to Bind Them	Susanne Hampton
Doctor...to Duchess?	Annie O'Neil
Second Chance with the Billionaire	Janice Maynard
Having Her Boss's Baby	Maureen Child

MILLS & BOON®
Large Print – August 2015

ROMANCE

The Billionaire's Bridal Bargain	Lynne Graham
At the Brazilian's Command	Susan Stephens
Carrying the Greek's Heir	Sharon Kendrick
The Sheikh's Princess Bride	Annie West
His Diamond of Convenience	Maisey Yates
Olivero's Outrageous Proposal	Kate Walker
The Italian's Deal for I Do	Jennifer Hayward
The Millionaire and the Maid	Michelle Douglas
Expecting the Earl's Baby	Jessica Gilmore
Best Man for the Bridesmaid	Jennifer Faye
It Started at a Wedding...	Kate Hardy

HISTORICAL

A Ring from a Marquess	Christine Merrill
Bound by Duty	Diane Gaston
From Wallflower to Countess	Janice Preston
Stolen by the Highlander	Terri Brisbin
Enslaved by the Viking	Harper St. George

MEDICAL

A Date with Her Valentine Doc	Melanie Milburne
It Happened in Paris...	Robin Gianna
The Sheikh Doctor's Bride	Meredith Webber
Temptation in Paradise	Joanna Neil
A Baby to Heal Their Hearts	Kate Hardy
The Surgeon's Baby Secret	Amber McKenzie

0715 GEN STD LP

MILLS & BOON®

Why shop at millsandboon.co.uk?

Each year, thousands of romance readers find their perfect read at millsandboon.co.uk. That's because we're passionate about bringing you the very best romantic fiction. Here are some of the advantages of shopping at www.millsandboon.co.uk:

* **Get new books first**—you'll be able to buy your favourite books one month before they hit the shops

* **Get exclusive discounts**—you'll also be able to buy our specially created monthly collections, with up to 50% off the RRP

* **Find your favourite authors**—latest news, interviews and new releases for all your favourite authors and series on our website, plus ideas for what to try next

* **Join in**—once you've bought your favourite books, don't forget to register with us to rate, review and join in the discussions

Visit **www.millsandboon.co.uk**
for all this and more today!